pc 8/24/78.

THE FLIGHT OF THE FOX

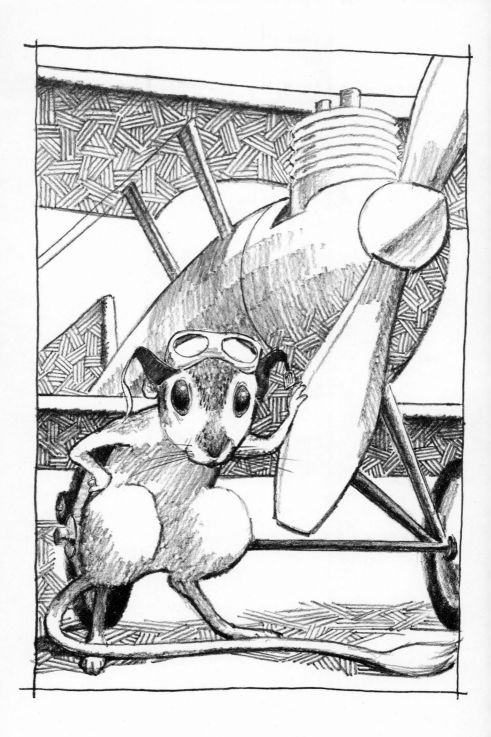

Shirley Rousseau Murphy

———

THE FLIGHT
OF
THE *FOX*

*Drawings by Don Sibley based on
original designs by Richard Cuffari*

NEW YORK *Atheneum* 1978

The discussion of starlings bullying bluebirds beginning on page 66
is from the U.S. Department of Agriculture Bulletin No. 868, as
quoted in "A Plague of Starlings," by Robert Cantwell, in *Sports
Illustrated*, Sept. 9, 1974 (pp. 107–118).

Library of Congress Cataloging in Publication Data

Murphy, Shirley Rousseau.
  The flight of the fox.

  SUMMARY: With the help of his friends, Rory, a
wandering kangaroo rat, restores a model of a Fairey Fox
airplane to fly on his travels and foils a flock of
starlings that has overrun the town.
  I. Cuffari, Richard, 1925–   II. Title.
PZ7.M956Fl   [Fic]   78–5436
ISBN 0–689–30662–8

For my husband, PATRICK J. MURPHY.
And especially for our nephew, MATT KILEY,
whose grandfather learned to fly the same way Rory did.

THE FLIGHT OF THE FOX

CHAPTER

I

THE train slowed beside the woods, ready to enter the town of Skrimville. The door of one freight car stood open two inches, and in this crack a mouselike figure stood, knees bent, his body poised to jump. As the engine braked, his tail twitched and his ears flattened in readiness. He tossed out his canvas pack, watched it roll down the steep embankment, then suddenly he leaped after it, tail swinging.

He landed rolling, paws over whiskery face, and fetched up against some pinecones. He stood, brushed himself off, and watched the train roar by above him. When it had gone, dragging its noise behind, he retrieved his pack and climbed up the embankment, sneezing at the smoke and rubbing his bruised backside. "There ought to be a better way to travel," he muttered irritably. Well at least he'd had the boxcar all to himself, except for that stretch between Rutledge and Vicksville when those two tramps got on. Then he'd had to stay hidden under the straw so as not to call attention to himself. He'd like to have told those two what he thought of their tobacco chewing

3

and spitting into the straw right beside him, but he never talked to people. Too risky.

He stood between the hot metal tracks staring toward the town ahead, then surveyed the countryside around him. His six-inch height didn't let him see too far, even from the raised embankment. He leaped up twice, as high as a man's head, and could see more. His leaps were like explosions, propelled by his strong hind legs.

He was much bigger than a mouse. He had hind legs like a kangaroo, and short front legs with sharp elbows. His fur was tan, his face tough and shrewd. His tail was extremely long and skinny, with a white tuft at the end like a dish mop. The old, worn pack he carried had obviously seen many miles. He continued to study the countryside with interest, for except for the one small town he could see no other houses; and that pleased him. People were all right in their places, but Rory didn't like to be crowded. What was that beyond those low hills? Another part of the town? He glanced at the trees that grew beside the embankment, then exploded suddenly in a leap that carried him halfway up the nearest pine, where he clung a moment, then climbed quickly until he could command a really good view of the surrounding land.

"Nope, no more houses," he said with satisfaction. "Just open fields. And that's an airport over there!" He gazed off toward the hangar and landing strip that lay beyond the town. "Not as big as Turbine Field, though." There was a Cessna 150, an old Navion, and a nice new Cougar there at the end. "But why is it

4

so flappin' quiet?" There should have been some activity, people walking around, a plane taking off. "There's not even a car parked by the hangar," he said, perplexed. "Why, that airfield looks like a flappin' morgue! And what the heck are those things lined up along the runway?" They looked like cannon. Six cannon. "Well my gosh, they sure are cannon! Now why would anyone put cannon beside an airstrip? Well, no accounting for humans," he said, twitching his whiskers.

That looked like the town dump there beside the runway. "Nice big dump," he muttered, pleased. He hurried down the tree and shouldered his pack. "A good dump, a good camp." He headed along between the tracks at a fast clip, thinking of a warm fire and a hot meal. He'd had nothing for breakfast but some cold beans.

2

THE kangaroo rat traveled along the raised railroad track until it came close to the town. Then he left it to strike off through the high grass, around the town's outskirts. His view from the raised track had been enough to see a dog or cat approaching, but now he could see nothing but the tall grass through which he pushed. He wasn't unduly concerned, though, and went along at his ease. The grass bent down with the weight of its seed and smelled fine. He found a trail that other animals had used, probably mice and moles. He followed it, pausing occasionally to leap high above the grass, making sure he was keeping in the right direction. And all the time he kept listening; there were people sounds from the town to his left, but nothing from the airfield.

It was well past noon when Rory arrived at a little muddy road and could see the dump just ahead. He strode along swinging his pack and skirting the deep tire tracks made by trash and garbage trucks. A thin bike track showed up in the mud here and there. The sun was warm on his back, and the silence of the dump suited him. It was entirely quiet except for the harsh arguing of a flock of birds somewhere farther on. As the path entered the dump, it was plunged into shadow by the mountains of trash, the cliffs of piled-up rusted cars and refrigerators and washing machines that towered on both sides. Limp bike tires hung down like dead snakes, and stained lampshades tilted rakishly. He wandered along the winding path looking for a possible camp and keeping an eye out for anything of value. The smells of the dump were familiar and comfortable. Old crankcase grease, sodden leather, sticky paint cans, rotten rubber, mildew. And new grass, for wherever dirt could collect in a dented fender or on top a refrigerator, bright green grass had sprouted. And wherever a dent held rain water, red rust ran down fresh as blood.

He made his way among smashed dolls and broken mop handles, poking into old cars and dark niches. He found three pennies under a worn boot and a good knife blade sticking out of the mud. He noted with satisfaction the abundance of mushrooms and dandelion greens. And there was no rotting garbage to take his appetite. He climbed a mountain of worn tires and could see the garbage dump farther on and could smell it on the breeze. It was covered with a flock of dark, quarreling birds busily engorging garbage. And what was that down there at the turn of the path? It looked like a piano crate. Rory descended in three leaps. Yes, a piano crate all right, huge and nearly empty of trash. Primfoggle Piano Company was stenciled on its side. A fellow could make a real mansion in a place like that if he was so inclined.

But Rory wasn't inclined. Just a few days rest and he'd be off. Up toward Allensville, he thought, now the weather was warm. He stood admiring the crate, though, until the breeze changed and he smelled berries and followed the smell at once.

The blackberry tangle was at the far side of the dump, its vines snaking through truck tires and over moldy sofas. The earliest berries were ripe. Rory picked a few and ate them as he wandered. When he saw the turned-over Buick, he stopped to look her over, for she was really an old-timer. "Nineteen twenty-eight or twenty-nine! They really built 'em in those days." The Buick lay on its back with its wheels in the air like a capsized beetle. It's roof was partly buried in the mud. Its hood was suspended some three feet off the ground, making a dark cave underneath.

There was a hole in the rear window. Rory slipped in and stood in the dim interior, his muddy feet making prints on the upholstered ceiling. The steering wheel towered above his head. Some stuffing had fallen down out of the seat. The windows were all so cracked he couldn't see much through them. Just shades of dark and light. The milky, shattered glass made the shadow under the hood look darker, except for a large, pale shape. "Likely some trash," Rory said, thinking the shape looked like a crouching cat. "Guess I'd better check, though." He slipped out the hole in the rear window and around to the Buick's windshield, to stand in the shadows and peer into the darkened cave.

And what he saw was not a cat, nor anything like a cat. There beneath the ancient Buick was a sight that made Rory catch his breath in amazement, made his heart pound wildly with desire.

CHAPTER

3

RORY stood staring into the darkness beneath the
Buick's suspended hood. He couldn't believe what he
saw. And when he did believe it, he poked himself to
see if he was dreaming.

Ever since that winter at Turbine Field he had
wished, at really wild moments—wished . . .

"My gosh," he breathed, "it's a plane! It's a model
plane!" Right in front of him, broken and rust-cov-
ered, lay tilted in the mud a real beauty of a biplane
with at least a four-foot wingspan. The U-control
wires were still sticking out of her wing. He walked
around her. He could see his reflection in the cracked
windshield almost as if there were a pilot sitting in the
cockpit. He wondered if he could get her upright, to
stand straight. He put his weight under the mud-cov-
ered wingtip and heaved. Sure enough, she straightened right up and stood jauntily.

There was a jagged hole in her fuselage. Her
propeller was gone; her upper right wing was partly
crushed. Her red and white paint was liberally
streaked with rust dripping down from the Buick,

and her smashed cowling lay in the mud. But she was a honey all the same. And her engine was in one piece. Even the spark plug was still perched on top, a quarter-inch-long white plug with *Champion* printed on its base. Rory stared at the plane, and stared. He thought and considered and scratched his chin.

"I could carve a new prop," he said hesitantly. "I could patch that wing and fix the body. Oh, it's crazy! *Crazy!*" His whiskers twitched with excitement. "I'd need glue and the right kind of paper, but with a whole dump I'm bound to find something. I'd need tools. Well, dumps have tools!" He began to grin. "I'm getting old and silly," he muttered. He examined her tires and her motor. He climbed up onto her lower wing and looked inside the cockpit. "I could cut holes in the firewall for cables, make rudder pedals . . ." And as he poked and investigated, Rory's crazy dream grew until already in his crotchety old mind the plane stood complete before him. Complete, and ready to fly.

It was then, right in the middle of his wild dream that he heard the birds in the garbage dump screaming hysterically and saw the sky darken as the flock raced toward him, dove low overhead, and began to circle just beyond him. They were after something, a dog or cat likely. Rory slipped out and climbed the trash heap behind the Buick until he could see what was going on.

It was a kid on a bike. The birds were having a regular fit, swooping down at the boy's head, and the boy trying to ignore them but ducking every few minutes as some bird came on stronger and nearly hit him. Rory watched, fascinated. He didn't like birds much, but he liked humans less. And this was some spectacle. "Why, those flappin' birds are *starlings!*" he muttered under his breath, scowling. Big purple-black birds with short tails, yellow beaks, and mean expressions. "I don't need a flock of starlings all over the place! There ain't a nastier-tempered bird . . ."

Well he didn't need a kid around either. Sure as shooting the kid would find that plane—unless the starlings drove him off. Rooting for the starlings, Rory slipped back to the Buick, dragged some rags and papers in to hide the plane, then went around through the dump and up another trash mountain and hid himself behind a bent baby buggy where he could look right out on the boy and the diving birds.

The kid was still trying to ignore the birds. He had leaned his bike against a jumble of tractor parts and was untying a cage from the bike rack. *A cage!* If the kid messed around with cages, you could bet he was the kind who set traps. Rory hated traps with a passion.

The boy fooled around for some time but did not remove the cage from the bike until the starlings, growing bored at last, perhaps because he ignored them, began to leave. They flew heavily off in twos and threes, then by dozens, back to the garbage dump, where Rory could hear them commencing to quarrel again. Now the boy, obviously relieved at the birds' departure, set the cage on top an old washing machine in a patch of sunshine, then went off to scrounge through the dump. Rory watched him. He would set aside an object now and then, a pitchfork with no handle, a bucket with a small hole. If the kid was scrounging junk, maybe he wasn't so bad. Rory leaned closer to see the cage and began to wonder what all that stuff on the bottom of it was. Looked like some lettuce leaves, a piece of chocolate cake, a lump of fur. *A lump of fur?* About that time the lump of fur moved, rolled over, and sat up, and Rory could see it was an animal about his own size, very fat, and very young.

It wasn't a mouse, it was far too big for a mouse. And too short-legged and too fat. It had practically no tail, just a stub. It had no ears that Rory could see. And hardly any nose, either. It was just a lump of an animal, but its eyes were bright and alert as it watched the boy. Pretty soon it leaned back against the cage, exposing its fat belly to the sun, closed its eyes, and seemed to doze off. Rory snorted. The young creature ought to be trying to get *out* of that cage, not lying there enjoying it!

The boy found an armature wound with copper wire and came back all excited to lay it beside the cage. "That thing's worth plenty!" he told the napping animal, who opened its eyes briefly and seemed to smile. Well the kid was scrounging junk to sell, then. Rory approved of that, it showed enterprise.

Pretty soon the kid sat down on a barrel next to the cage and took a sandwich out of his pocket. Rory's stomach growled with hunger. He'd forgotten all about making a fire and cooking his noon meal, and the day was getting on. The kid finished his sandwich and hauled out a chocolate bar, then began to talk to the furry lump as he fed it small bits of chocolate. "She didn't have to come barging in like that and find you. The old bat didn't have any business coming into my room with the door closed anyway! Dad wouldn't! I hope old Critch chokes! *Housekeeper!* Who needs a housekeeper! I would'a been fine by myself." The boy seemed almost on the verge of tears, and the young animal was standing up stretching its paws through the cage imploringly.

"You understand, don't you, Crispin?" The boy began to rub the animal's soft stomach. "And if I take you home again, she'll do what she said, you can bet on it. I thought she'd *already* killed you when she threw your cage out the door like that." He stared around the dump unhappily. "Got to find a place where you'll be safe. Some place where dogs and cats can't get in. Boy! Old Critch thought you were a rat! She'd never even heard of a lemming, the stupid woman!" The boy rose and adjusted the cage so it would remain in the sunshine. "I'll find a place, you'll see," and off he went around a pile of bed springs.

So that young animal was a lemming. Rory had some vague memory of hearing about lemmings—up in the far north where the snow was deep, he thought. He wanted to stay and talk to the lemming and to find out what the trouble was all about, but with the plane sitting there under the Buick, he knew he'd better follow that boy.

CHAPTER

4

RORY raced around the dump for some time keeping an eye on the kid. Once his foot slipped and he made a slight noise so the kid turned, puzzled, and studied the place where Rory crouched. But Rory kept well hidden and at last the boy went on.

The kid wasn't a bad-looking sort. He must be about twelve, Rory guessed, and had freckles. Rory hurried to catch up with him, slipping along behind him more openly until he was walking practically in the kid's shadow.

And, just as Rory had feared, he was heading right for the turned-over Buick.

The Buick seemed to fascinate the boy. He stood staring as if he enjoyed the sight of the wheels in the air. Rory scowled. The kid was far too close and far too interested. Rory picked up a rock and shied it at a tin can, ducking behind an old boot as the boy spun around wide-eyed.

The kid looked around, puzzled, then turned back once again to the Buick. Rory slipped around a jungle of trash and squeezed in through the Buick's back window. His heart was pounding with apprehension. He didn't know what he meant to do, but he sure wasn't going to let the kid have that plane. *His* plane! *Maybe he won't even see it*, he thought. *I covered it pretty good.* But knowing boys, he wouldn't bet on that.

The kid stood, hands in pockets, looking at the Buick. Then he knelt down and tried to peer in through the cracked windows. His face was only inches from Rory. Rory was pretty sure he couldn't see through into the darkness. To Rory, looking out into the light, the boy's head was a giant dark blob. Then the boy turned toward the Buick's suspended hood. Expecting the worst, Rory slipped quickly out. He wished he had some kind of weapon. The boy paused to stare at the ground, then touched something there in the mud. What was he looking at? Rory maneuvered around until he could see the ground, too.

The kid was staring at *footprints!* Rory's own flappin' footprints right there in the mud! The boy looked, then bent down to touch Rory's footprint with his finger. Then he cupped his hands and reached in toward the paper and rags Rory had piled in front of the plane as if he expected to catch an animal running out—the animal that had made those prints. All of a sudden he jerked the papers away, tensed to catch something—and stopped cold.

Drat! He's found my plane! Oh the flappin' dratted luck! He's found it and he'll be off with it sure as heck! Rory stared past the boy's pant legs at the plane, and in his moment of anguish he imagined her all shiny new and saw himself in the cockpit—*drat the kid!* He looked around for something to throw, anything.

"My gosh!" The kid breathed out loud. "My gosh, it's an old biplane, an old gas burner! Look at that engine!" He reached out to touch the engine and the tiny spark plug, much as Rory had done. "I've never even seen an engine like that. How long has this plane been here?" Kneeling under the Buick, the boy stared up at the hood over his head. "Well I've never seen the Buick, *it's* been dumped since spring vacation and I'll bet the plane has, too!"

Rory picked up some small bits of metal and pebbles from among the junk scattered around him. If the kid had turned around he'd have seen him, but he was so desperate now he didn't care. All he could think of was that lovely plane, his plane, of sitting in the cockpit. Of the propeller spinning and the plane lifting into the sky with him in command, flying between clouds, free on the wind . . . The boy was pulling more paper and rags away, examining the plane closely. "Man, I bet that engine's worth plenty." He took hold of the plane and began to lift her out.

Rory slung his pawful of pebbles as hard as he could at the boy's backside.

The kid dropped the plane like he'd been burned. He looked all around. But he saw nothing, and finally, puzzled but determined, he reached in again for the plane and this time he lifted it out.

Rory was beside himself. *It's my plane, you dratted kid!* he thought frantically. *You can't have her!* he wanted to shout, but he kept quiet. He picked up the biggest rock he could find and slipped around to where he could throw at an angle and not hurt the plane. And he let fly. He hit the boy in the side of the knee, and the boy yelped and jumped up, still clutching the plane.

Rory made sure he was well-hidden. If he didn't show himself, he just might be able to scare the daylights out of the kid. The boy knelt and picked up the rock that had hit him and stared all around trying to see where it had come from. This kid wasn't going to scare easy. There was only one other way Rory could think of to really scare him, and he hesitated to try that. The boy put the rock in his pocket and started down the path with the plane. I'm asking for trouble, Rory thought as he cupped his paws around his mouth. But in final desperation he made his voice as deep and loud as he could.

"Get your grubby hands off that plane!"

The kid froze.

Rory cupped his paws again. *"Put that plane down, you little thief! Put it back where you found it!"*

Now the boy looked scared. He knelt to put the plane back. Then all of a sudden he seemed to change his mind. He straightened up and stared around him, scowling. Then suddenly he shouted, "If you want this plane, come get it! I'm not leaving it for some coward who's too chicken to show himself!"

Drat the kid!

"Well?" If the boy was scared now, he didn't show it. He looked as angry as Rory felt. "Okay," he shouted at last, "If you won't talk and won't come out then it's my plane!" He started down the path again carrying the little biplane, carrying Rory's dream away with him.

Rory was so furious his tail twitched convulsively. What was he going to do? And then with sudden inspiration he shouted, "If you don't put it down, I'll toss this fat lemming of yours onto the garbage dump for the birds to peck, and I'll ram this cage over your head!"

The boy spun around, looking for the source of the voice.

"Are you going to put that plane back or am I going to take this lemming and . . ."

Hastily the boy set the plane back underneath the Buick, then stood defiantly in the center of the path. "Okay, give me the cage! Show yourself and give me the cage—*if* you have it! Just bring it on out here. And you'd better not hurt the lemming."

Rory knew if he didn't produce the cage the kid was going to take the plane anyway, and of course he didn't even have the cage. He had to distract the boy further.

"Where's my cage, you coward! *You're bluffing!*"

"I ain't bluffing, sonny!" Rory shouted. "You can—" but before Rory could finish, the boy dove across the path toward the tomato can, kicked the can aside, and snatched Rory up by the tail.

"I thought your voice was coming from there!" he said triumphantly as Rory dangled upside down, his pack flapping from his shoulders. All the blood was rushing to his head.

The boy stood dangling him and gawking. He examined Rory's tail, which he still held in a tight grip. He pulled out one hind leg and studied it. He was really very nosy. He peered into Rory's face and Rory scowled back at him. "Boy!" he said at last, "I never saw an animal like you in my whole life! And how come you're wearing a pack?" He fingered the pack and tried to look inside. Rory twisted away, indignant. "Well say something!" the boy said. "It was you talking, don't deny it!" He brought his face close to Rory's, looking into Rory's eyes. "Say something or I'll shake the life out of you!"

Rory was getting pretty dizzy with hanging upside down. The straps on his pack were cutting into his armpits. "Put me down, you little varmint, or I'll flip over and take a bite out of your hand that'll look like a major finger amputation!"

"If I put you down, you'll run off!"

Rory flipped over and had the kid's wrist in both paws and his mouth open to bite when the kid dropped him. He hit the ground on his big feet, thought of running, but knew if he did he'd lose the plane. Reluctantly, furiously, he turned to face the boy square on. "All right you little whelp, are you going to leave of your own accord or am I going to jump up and bite your nose for you?" Rory leaped right at the kid's face to demonstrate, and the surprised boy nearly fell over backward.

When Rory stood on the ground again, staring up, the boy just gaped down at him. "Well," Rory re-

peated, "are you going to leave my plane alone . . ."
He made ready to jump again.

"No, wait," the boy said. "Wait a minute." He just
kept staring at Rory. "This is crazy! I don't believe
this! You're wearing a pack, and you're talking!"

"So?"

"And—whatever you are—what makes you think
that's *your* plane? Stuff in the dump is anyone's prop-
erty. Finders—*oh!*" He frowned at Rory. "You mean
you'd already found it?"

"That's right, sonny. I'd found it. I claim salvage
rights on it, and that makes it my plane all right!"

The boy didn't seem frightened any more. He was
. . . *was he smiling?* Great flappin' rattlesnakes! The
dumb kid was grinning at him! "What're you laughing at!" Rory almost screamed. "What d'you think's
so funny!"

And suddenly the kid bent over double, laughing.

After a long while he straightened up and tried to
wipe the grin from his face.

"*Well? What's so flappin' funny!*"

"I just don't believe this. I just never saw a talking mouse before. Not one wearing a pack, and with
such an angry expression!"

"I ain't no *mouse*, sonny! I ain't no kind of *mouse!*"
Rory spat angrily over his left shoulder. "You have a
smart lip for a boy your age! You'd do well to keep
it buttoned."

"If you're not a mouse, what are you?"

"I'm a kangaroo rat! You show your ignorance by
not recognizing the fact."

22

I'd say he's his own lemming, sonny."

"Well I—well I . . ." Charlie didn't seem to know how to answer.

"Would you want to belong to someone, sonny? Be someone's pet boy?"

Charlie stared at the kangaroo rat. "Well . . . well I guess I wouldn't. Listen, if I brought him over here, would you talk to him? I'm really worried about him. I don't know if he can make it on his own."

"What's this all about, sonny? What're you doing out here in the dump with that youngster in a cage anyway?"

"It's the housekeeper. She made me bring him. I mean, she made me get him out of the house. She *threw* him out of the house! See, I had him hidden and . . ."

Rory settled back against the plane's tail assembly and smoothed his whiskers. "See here, sonny, maybe you'd better start at the beginning."

Charlie thought for a minute. "I'm not sure where the beginning is. It's all pretty complicated when you think about it."

"Well start with the housekeeper, then."

"Okay. Old Critch—Mrs. Critch. See, my dad hired her to keep house when he had to leave to go to work up at Snodly Field. Dad owns that mechanic's hangar over at the airfield, but it's all closed down, the whole field is closed. There isn't any business. So he had to go up to Snodley Field to work, and my mother is dead, so he hired Mrs. Critch to keep house. To look after me," Charlie said crossly. "She's really an old grump, but it was either her or Mrs. Larken and *she* wheezes. Well, so there we are, Mrs. Critch and me, and her grungy nephew visiting her sometimes, and it's really a lousy summer. Dad's away, the airfield's closed, and the dump—well, you saw those birds, I guess. Even the dump isn't like it used to be."

"Okay. So go on."

"Well, so last month my Uncle Joe came through Skrimville on his way home from fishing in Canada, and he brought me the lemming. He found him in his tent, hundreds of miles below where this kind of lemming lives, and he didn't want to turn him out all alone so he brought him to me. I kept him hidden under my bed until this morning. And this morning old Critch barged in and saw him and began shouting, 'It's a rat! It's a rat! All this greasy junk in your room and now you've got a rat in here! Get it out of here or I'll kill it!' Then she grabbed up the cage and ran down the hall with it and threw it right out the front door and I thought she'd already killed him."

In spite of himself, Rory was beginning to feel sorry for the kid, to say nothing of the young lemming. "Don't you have some friends who would keep him? He's pretty young to be off on his own."

"I know, that's what worries me. And all my friends are either out of town, or we've had a fight, like Jim Blakey. Or they have cats, like Nancy Reed. The only other kid in town is old Critch's nephew, Mush, and you can bet it was Mush who put her onto Crispin in the first place, snooping around my room when I wasn't there. He probably found the food I keep in my desk drawer. Good thing there's so much junk under my bed or he'd have found the cage, too."

"So," Rory said, "so now you've got to leave the youngster out here."

"I wish I could think of something else. Even the garage at our house isn't safe with old Critch hanging around it. I wish my dad were here. If Dad was here, he'd sent old Critch packing."

"You could call him, maybe—"

"He's got too much on his mind. It's been pretty hard on Dad since my mom died two years ago. And now with the business folded—well I just can't bother him. Besides, even if he told old Critch to let me keep Crispin, I'm not sure she'd do what he told her."

"Well, why is the airfield closed, sonny? Why would a town the size of this one close its airfield?"

"You saw those starlings diving around here awhile ago?"

"Sure did, sonny. Nasty birds. Why I've seen starlings attack other birds and drive them right out of the nest. They're the pestiest critters alive."

"They sure are. Well that flock of starlings came into Skrimville early last spring. They flocked all over the dump and the airfield, and every time a plane took off or landed they flew up and got in its way. They drove the pilots crazy. Then one day a little private jet sucked so many starlings into its jet mechanism that it crashed and four people were killed. Well, right away the city closed the airfield, and it hasn't been open since."

"But didn't they try to get rid of the starlings? A whole town—"

"Oh, they tried. They tried everything. But those birds aren't afraid of much. Someone tried driving a car down the runway honking its horn before a plane took off, to scare the birds away. That worked for about two days, then the birds got used to it. Then the mayor bought those war surplus cannon to fire off blanks to scare them, but the starlings got used to that, too."

"Did they try to poison them? Seems mean, but sometimes—"

"They put out poison pellets and a few starlings died, then those crazy birds learned to avoid the pellets, and the town picked them all up again so no little kid or dog would get them."

"Well maybe shotguns . . ."

"Oh, people tried shooting them but pretty soon the starlings started avoiding anyone with a gun. They'd just fly off. And people in town complained about all the noise. The mayor even bought a loudspeaker and sent for a recording of starling distress calls from a museum in Washington. He mounted the loudspeaker on his car so he could drive out and play the record in the dump in the daytime, then drive back and play it in town at night when the birds came in to roost. That worked fine for a while, the birds were really jittery and couldn't settle down. Everyone thought they'd leave. But gradually they got used to it and didn't pay any more attention. And the distress calls were so awful that everyone in town was more jittery than the birds.

"So Skrimville Field is closed. My dad's repair shop is closed. Dad is living up in Allensville in a boarding house, working for someone else. Mrs. Critch is living in our spare room. And even the dump is miserable. Without Crispin it would really have been a lousy summer, and now . . ." Charlie stared at Rory, and Rory stared back. The kid was making Rory feel pretty bad.

"How come you named the lemming Crispin?" Rory asked softly, just for something to say to the boy.

"It's funny about that. I was trying to think what to name him. I went to sleep trying to decide between Herman and Louie and Rover. And in the morning when I woke up, I just said *Crispin* like it came right out of the blue. And the little beggar jumped off the pillow onto my chest and stuck his nose in my face as if he knew his name right off."

Rory smiled. This was getting more interesting every minute. "Well go on, sonny, go get that lemming and let's see what he has to say for himself."

6

CHARLIE found Crispin asleep in the patch of sunshine that splashed across the floor of his cage. His short paws were wrapped around the chocolate cake as if he'd stuffed himself and fallen asleep before he finished. Charlie carried the cage back to the Buick and set it down in front of the kangaroo rat. Crispin, sated with food, did not stir. He snored softly, and his distended stomach gurgled now and then.

The kangaroo rat studied the sleeping lemming, the snub nose, the nearly invisible ears, the short legs and half-inch tail. "Ain't very well equipped, is he?" Rory said, fingering his own large ears and flicking his long tail so the white ruff arched high over his head. "And who ever heard—who *ever* heard of hair on the bottoms of your feet!"

"Well *you* have hair between your toes!" Charlie challenged. "Look at it, it's a regular mat of hair!"

"My hair," Rory said, extending his toes to show the matted hair between them, "is for walking on sand. It has a purpose. And it's not on the bottoms of my feet."

"*His* hair," Charlie growled back, "is for walking on ice! It's to keep from slipping! You try walking on ice with those slick feet of yours and see what happens!"

Crispin woke then, stared at Rory, and began to twitch his whiskers.

"Awake now, sonny? So you're a lemming, are you? Do you speak English?"

Crispin stared at Rory, glanced up uneasily at Charlie, then back at the kangaroo rat. He remained silent.

"It's all right, sonny. You don't have to say a thing if you don't want to."

The lemming pushed as close to Rory as he could against the bars of his cage, and whispered, "How come *you're* talking? We're not supposed to talk to people!" He stared over his shoulder at Charlie. "Charlie's my friend and I've *wanted* to talk to him *lots* of times. But I never did! Well, not so he knew about it."

"It's all right, sonny. Old Charlie here won't say anything." The kangaroo rat glanced at Charlie as if Charlie hadn't better say anything. "And your name's Crispin, sonny! That right?"

"Yes sir," said the lemming.

"Well I'm Rory from Cricket Run, Arizona, on my way to see the world."

The lemming seemed impressed. Charlie was impressed, too, because Arizona was a long way from Skrimville.

"Is Crispin your only name, sonny? If Charlie named you Crispin, didn't you have another name

before that? What did your mother call you?"

"Oh, Charlie didn't name me Crispin. That's always been my name."

"Of course I named you!" Charlie interrupted. "Don't you remember, I went to sleep thinking of names, and when I woke up I named you Crispin."

"But *you* didn't name me that, Charlie," said the lemming stubbornly. "You just thought you did. See, when you started trying names on me—*Rover!*—Well I just stood all I could. *I* didn't want to be called Rover! I didn't even like *Louie.* So when you went to sleep I sat by your ear and whispered my real name over and over. I sat there all night, just whispering, and when you woke up"—the lemming smiled a joyful smile—"when you woke up, you knew what my name was, Charlie. You knew right away!"

Charlie stared at the lemming. He couldn't believe it. He'd been *trained* by a *lemming!* "But why didn't you just *tell* me your name? You could have talked to me."

"I'd *never* talked to a person, Charlie. At home they told us—Mama said you should never, never talk to a person, that it was the worst thing you could do."

"Well I wouldn't have *told* anyone!"

"How was I to know? Anyone who would keep a person in a cage all the time."

"Oh, come on, you're the one who always wants to get back in the cage where the food is." (At that moment there was still a fig bar, two grapes, and the slept-on chocolate cake.)

"But you could have left the door open. I didn't

36

like it much with the door closed." The lemming had raised up on his hind legs and was staring defiantly at Charlie.

"If I'd left the door open and you'd got out and Mrs. Critch had found you, you'd be a dead duck. A dead lemming. I kept you in there for your own good. I let you out at night, didn't I? I let you sleep with me."

Crispin ignored this. Still rearing, he had begun to chitter. His voice rose, his eyes flashed, and his teeth showed white and sharp. He looked nothing like the gentle, soft lemming of a moment before. When he began to jump up and down, Rory looked really amazed. "Excitable little fellow, ain't he?"

"He does that sometimes. One minute all sweetness, and the next minute a regular tantrum. He's bitten me twice."

"Maybe he belongs in a cage. Are they all like that?"

"I guess so. I read about them in a book. It said they go kind of crazy sometimes. So crazy they even drown themselves."

"Oh, come now, sonny! No animal's dumb enough to drown himself. A human, maybe. But not an animal."

"Lemmings do, though. Every few years, as soon as spring comes, they crawl up out of the snow where they've been sleeping and go stampeding off, thousands of them. They eat every blade of grass in their way, and nothing can stop them; they go right over houses, or right through them. They'd run over a man

37

if he stood still. No one knows what makes them do it. When they get to the ocean they just keep going, straight in. They swim until they can't swim any more, then they drown." Charlie remembered how impolite it is to talk about someone in front of him and glanced at Crispin. But Crispin didn't seem to have heard. He was still chittering.

"They show up on the tundra so suddenly," Charlie continued, "that some people think they fall out of the sky. Or blow there on the wind. And some people think they're searching for the lost continent of Atlantis. They're really famous, but still no one knows why they drown themselves."

The kangaroo rat considered Crispin. "Is any of that stuff true, sonny?"

Crispin stopped chittering and gave Rory a beatific look. "*I* don't know. I never *heard* of Atlantis. And I never was up in the sky. Though I think about it sometimes," he said dreamily. He had forgotten his anger completely. "It was cold up in Canada. There was twelve feet of snow over our tunnel last winter. When spring came and the snow started to melt, oh my, we all just raced out." He sighed. "We did have a wonderful run, we ran for days. No one thought of stopping. I never *meant* to *drown* myself. When we came to the water we just all plunged in. I kept thinking the shore would come pretty soon, but it never did. Then everything went black."

"Then that *is* what happened to you," Charlie said. "I always wondered. See," he said to Rory, "my uncle never could figure out how he got down into southern Canada. But you didn't swim all that way," he said to the lemming. He lifted Crispin out of his cage. "You couldn't have swum that far south. And how did you keep from drowning, if everything went black?"

CHARLIE nudged Crispin. "How did you get so far south?" he repeated. "How did you get out of the ocean if everything went black?"

The lemming stared up at Charlie. "This old muskrat, he pulled me out, Charlie. He said he swam over a mile, dragging me to shore. He pumped the water out of me and took care of me. I stayed there a long time. Then when I felt better, I decided to travel. Muskrats live mostly on tules and cattails, and I was tired of *that*. I just kept going where it was warmest, I guess. I suppose I was going south. I didn't care much for the snow and ice, and I'd never seen the world. I'd spent all my life under that snow. I was tired of other lemmings, too. They're so *excitable*. There was a whole world out there, coming south. A whole world . . ." The lemming went off dreaming again. Charlie and Rory looked at each other, and grinned. "A whole world . . ." The lemming repeated.

"But how come my uncle found you inside his

tent?" Charlie insisted. "What were you doing in there?"

"Because of the cornbread and bacon," Crispin said longingly. "I could smell such a wonderful smell coming to me in the night where I was sleeping in a log. I just went out and followed it. I went in the tent where it was, and I ate and ate, and then I went to sleep. I woke up once because the man began to snore. I didn't know he was a *man*, he was just a big, snoring animal with clothes on. His snoring sounded like my cousins sleeping all around me, only louder. It was soothing, and I went back to sleep. Then when I woke up the next time, I was in a box with holes in it. I was on my way to you, Charlie." The lemming gave Charlie such a loving look that you'd never know he'd been rocking with rage only moments before. But then he seemed to recollect himself, and his expression became very sad. "And now—and now . . ." he said, a tear sliding down his furry cheek, "and now you're going to abandon me."

"But I . . ."

The lemming began crying pitifully. He hiccuped as he looked up at Charlie. "I *liked* it at your house, Charlie. I *liked* sleeping on your pillow and getting under the bed and pulling out the stuffing and chewing on your socks. And I liked all the things we did together, going in the garden when old hatchet face was gone, eating the petunias . . ."

"*I* didn't eat the petunias," Charlie said crossly. The lemming had made him feel just terrible. He stared at Rory hopelessly. He guessed he would be abandoning the lemming if he left him in the dump.

The kangaroo rat twitched a whisker and tried not to smile. He had begun to get a really stupendous idea. There was a long silence while the sun shone down on the rust and metal and new grass, while the starlings quarreled over garbage, and the summer breeze tickled the animals' fur. Rory studied Charlie appraisingly, and at last he smoothed his whiskers, cleared his throat, and said softly, "Maybe I could help you out, sonny."

Charlie stared at the kangaroo rat, at the purposeful expression in those dark eyes. Somehow, the animal's words made him uneasy. "How could you help me?" he said slowly.

Rory looked back, taking stock of the boy, and then he made his pitch. "I might," he said casually, "I *might* look out for the youngster—if you were to do me a favor in return."

The lemming sat quietly. He listened to Charlie and the kangaroo rat. They talked for a long time. He didn't understand all the words they used, words like propeller and points and speedskin, like spark plugs and screwdrivers, but he knew he was listening to his reprieve. He knew there would be someone to take care of him. He leaned back against the side of his cage with his belly exposed and chittered happily to himself.

8

AS THE afternoon cooled and the sun dimmed, the young lemming climbed the trash mountain behind the Buick, then climbed up onto a rusted radiator right at the top. He was free. He stared out at the world and at the wide sky overhead, then down to where Rory was working on the plane. It was comforting to have Rory near, fiddling with a motor as he had seen Charlie do so many times—though he did miss Charlie.

The wind tickled his whiskers. The last rays of the sun warmed his stomach. He could see fields stretching away and see woods beyond and see the town where he had lived with Charlie. Strange how the houses looked so small. Little bitty things clustered there, yet when you were in one, it seemed as big as the whole world. Well he had no house or cage to shut him in now. He shivered with the enormity of his freedom and hunkered down closer to the radiator. He had been a long time shut inside, and now so much space all at once made him a little uneasy.

And he did feel lost without Charlie Gribble. The

kangaroo rat was very gruff and short-tempered and expected a person to stay awake all the time.

Well, Charlie would be back soon. He had promised. He would come with the engine parts Rory wanted, with the balsa wood and paper and glue and all the strange things that would somehow make the plane fly. Rory had said, "I'll take good care of the young lemming, Charlie Gribble. And you'll pick up my supplies at the hobby shop."

"I'll bring the stuff out tomorrow."

"Alone. No friends tagging along."

"Yes, alone."

Crispin smelled the new grass that grew out of the radiator, and the smell had a wildness about it that made him shiver again. He sniffed the smells that came from the dump itself, the scents of rust and burned cloth and old grease. The old grease was the most comforting, because it smelled like the nuts and bolts and machine parts in Charlie's room. He looked at some mallow weeds growing up tall as young trees. He saw the way the berry bushes were loaded with ripening berries. He looked down at Rory there beside the Buick; and when Rory called him, he climbed down to help.

"There, sonny! Get behind that wing and push for all you're worth."

Crispin pushed, and Rory pushed, and the plane began to move slowly down the muddy path.

They had to manuever to keep her away from the puddles so she wouldn't get stuck, and clear the path of old shoes and mop handles as they went. But eventually they had pushed the plane along through the dump to where the big piano crate stood, cleaned the rubbish out of it, swept the floor, then backed the plane in.

Crispin stood inside the hangar staring up in awe at the big plane. Could Rory really fly it? It looked very ragged and old with the tear in its wing and the hole in its body. The wheels were so caked with mud, the paint so streaked and rusty. The windshield was bleary with cracks and with age. But still, Crispin thought, puzzling, in spite of all that the plane seemed somehow grand, towering there.

"When we have a propeller," Rory said, "she'll make a wind like you never felt, sonny. And she'll fly on that wind, she'll make a kind of magic you can't even imagine. Up there," he said, gesturing toward the sky. "Up there, away from muddy roads and stinking freight trains and dogs and cats and humans. Like you cut a cord that tied you to the earth. Like you're a bloomin' bird up there!"

Crispin looked out at the starlings perched on a refrigerator, and past them to the pale sunset. Pretty soon maybe he would be flying up there, higher than those birds ever had.

As the sun lowered, people in Skrimville began to prepare for the night. Women rushed to bring in their wash; lawn chairs were stowed in garages; children were called indoors; cars were covered or put under shelter. Then, all preparations made, Skrimville pulled its shades, turned on its TVs, and tried to ignore the soft summer evening as the starlings descended like a black cloud to roost on every available surface.

For several weeks after they first came the starlings had roosted each night in the pine grove south of town. Under their weight the branches of the pines had broken. Now the birds had taken to roosting in the town itself, rows and rows of them shouldering each other out of the way along the rooftops and sign boards and electrical and telephone wires, quarreling loudly and dirtying everything beneath them. Skrimville had had to reinforce all the wires and put on two extra crews of street cleaners, and schemes to drive the starlings from the dump had been forgotten as everyone concentrated on trying to drive them out of town. When all schemes had failed, Skrimville had subsided into a state of sullen depression.

CHAPTER

9

I T W A S sunset when Rory paused in his work and stood admiring the hangar. Two cots now stood along the wall, and a worktable, with tools hung up behind it: some broken hacksaw blades, half a scissors, a cracked ruler, a whole needle, razor blades carefully cleaned of rust, some pencils, and two valuable C-clamps he had found. A pile of fairly clean rags lay folded on the table. And towering over table and cots, taking up most of the hangar, the plane shone brightly now that her rust had been scrubbed away.

In front of the hangar the lemming had laid a campfire ready in an old hubcap. Rory searched for matches, then went to light it. The youngster was off somewhere gathering mushrooms, dandelions and berries for supper. Rory had just struck flame to tinder when he felt a terrible wind and the sky went dark. A cloud of birds swept low above him, its passage snuffing the flame and tearing at his whiskers. Then, as suddenly, it was gone, flapping off toward the town. The harsh voices and off-key whistles faded in the distance.

Rory stared after the flock. He had been ignoring the fact of the starlings all day. But you could hardly ignore that screaming flight. "Well, most birds mind their own business," he muttered, knowing very well that starlings never mind their own business.

Crispin, coming around the corner with an armful of mushrooms, dropped his burden and scrambled up the nearest trash heap to watch the flock grow smaller then drop suddenly down over Skrimville. "They used to come over Charlie's house like that, Rory. Sometimes they used to stare in the window at me and hiss, and I never knew what they wanted."

"Why does that fool town put up with them?"

"They've tried to get rid of them, Rory. They've tried all kinds of things, I heard on Charlie's radio. They talked and talked about it. But nothing ever works."

"Well they just haven't thought of the right thing. Come on, sonny, bring those mushrooms and let's get supper started."

As they prepared their supper, Rory told Crispin about last winter, living in the Turbine Field hangar. He had learned a lot in that hangar, watching the mechanics tear down planes and fix them. He told Crispin how the chief mechanic's wife used to send down a plate of fudge occasionally, and Rory would almost die before everyone else left it long enough for him to slip out from behind the stove and snatch a piece or two.

"Almost caught me once. I tripped on a gasket and went tail over teacup right into a can of screws, scat-

tered them from one end of that hangar to the other. Good thing I was right behind the mechanic's heels, because he thought he'd kicked it over himself. I hit for that stove and didn't come out for three days. I never lived in a real house, though, like you, sonny. The closest I ever came to that was when I holed up under the couch in a Samaritan Rescue Mission during a terrible rain. Hoo, boy, those old winos could tell the stories. But I haven't been able to stand the smell of wine since, because one night an old boy shoved his jug under the sofa right next to where I was sleeping. I had to have a taste, of course. Boy, sonny, that was some night.

"But tell me how it was, living in a real house. Tell me how it was at Charlie Gribble's."

"It was grand, Rory. Charlie made these neat little sandwiches for me, anchovies and peanut butter and pickles. And when Mrs. Critch went shopping, Charlie took me out in the yard and let me eat wild mint and petunias and lie in the damp grass." Crispin sighed. "But sometimes, sitting there in my cage under the bed in the middle of the day, all alone, I used to think about being off by myself again in the world, running along under the leaves in the wind, finding adventure. And sometimes, there in the dark, I'd think about the sky and the birds I could see from Charlie's window. That must be something, to be sailing around up there. I always wondered if it didn't make them giddy. Will it make *us* giddy, Rory, flying around like that? What's it like, up in the sky? Have you ever *flown* in an airplane before? Will I sit in the back cockpit, or the front one? Where will we go, Rory? Can you see the whole world from up there?"

"We might see the whole world, sonny. A little at a time. It'll be flappin' great up there, in the clouds —on the wind . . ." Rory sat twirling the tuft of his tail, thinking. The lemming was very young, very eager. Rory tried to remember how he had felt at that age. That was a long time ago. He guessed he had been pretty eager, too. He could remember his mother, when he was younger than Crispin, leaning over his bed in the underground cave while the hot desert wind blew down from above. He could remember her tucking him in at night and telling him the stars were shining, up above the sand. He could remember her bringing him yucca root and cactus pears when he was sick, and—well, he could remember a lot of things, when he tried. He guessed maybe he'd better give a little thought to the care and feeding of young lemmings. *I'm taking on something*, Rory thought, *raising a youngster*. It had been a long time since he had had to account for anyone but himself.

Crispin began to doze. The fire threw long shadows into the darkness. Rory contemplated the good supper they had had and felt a sudden quiet pleasure in the circumstances that had brought him here.

At last he carried the sleeping lemming to bed, then climbed into his own cot and lay looking up at the black silhouette of the plane that towered over them, her wide double wings slightly lifted, and he could hardly believe what he had set out to do. Maybe his

51

dream was only a dream. Maybe he would never fly her.

"*Well I'm flappin' well going to try! No, not try! We're going to* do *it! Just you see if we don't!*" he said softly to the darkness. And then he turned over and slept.

———

CHARLIE GRIBBLE liked buying things at the hobby shop when he had the money, which was seldom. But now he was loaded because the kangaroo rat had pulled a wad of bills out of his pack and handed it to him with the supply list.

"I've never seen a pawful of money like that!" Charlie had said, staring.

"You'd be surprised how much of that money I've found, sonny. Quarters and dimes, a dollar bill, even a five or ten sometimes. People are a pretty careless lot. And if the owner's gone and lost it, I don't feel bad about picking it up. If I didn't, someone else would, and I can't hardly go running down the street shouting, '*Who lost this dollar bill?*' can I?

Charlie grinned. "No, I guess you can't."

"Then, some of that money came from scrounging stuff in dumps and selling it, same as you. I even found a diamond ring once, down inside the motor housing of an old washing machine. I can tell a real diamond, sonny, and that sure was a beauty."

"But how do you sell stuff like that? I thought you

didn't like talking to people."

"I don't need to talk to people. I just carry whatever I have through the mail slot or a window—at night, of course—and I leave a note asking the pawnbroker or the junk salesman to put the money in an envelope, under the door. I suppose I get the short end of the deal sometimes, but in my case, sonny, it's about the only comfortable way to do business. Now, all this stuff you're going to buy for me—if you hadn't come along I'd have had to slip it out of the store at night and leave the cash, and some of those things are pretty big to be slippin' out through the mail slot. I'm glad we met up, sonny. This arrangement is going to work just fine."

Now Charlie entered Hobie's Hobby Shop with a fist full of green clutched against Rory's list. The list read:

> *One small hammer*
> *Three screwdrivers, assorted*
> *Exacto Knife*
> *Small crescent wrench*
> *Two D flashlight batteries*
> *One toggle switch*
> *Five pairs small brass hinges, with screws*
> *Balsa wood: ¼" stringers, two sheets ⅛"*
> *Paint: one jar white, one jar red*
> *Thinner*
> *Paint brushes, one small, one medium*
> *Airplane glue*
> *Airplane paper*

54

hangar; the cots, the worktable, the array of tools, and the blue cashmere blankets Crispin had cut from a dog-chewed sweater. The plane looked great with the rust scrubbed off. Charlie watched Rory root through the hobby shop bag until he found the small tools. The kangaroo rat fished out a wrench and a screwdriver, then began to dismantle the clock he had found. The animal's forearms were not very long, nor did they seem to be the strongest part of him. But Rory threw all his weight onto the wrench again and again until he had the rusty gears removed. Charlie hunkered down beside him to watch.

"Going to rig up a dashboard control with these gears, sonny. So I can control the needle valve, control the gas going into the engine. But I'm not sure," Rory said, pausing to wrench free a particularly stubborn gear, "I'm not sure these gears are big enough. Have to give them a try, but . . ." he trailed off, took several more turns with the screwdriver, growled, "Flappin' rust!" Then put the whole thing down and stared up at Charlie. "Did you get everything on that list, sonny? I didn't see no propeller in there."

"I got everything but the propeller and the plugs and points. Hobie had to order the propeller; he said it might be in next week. The plugs and points are going to be harder. Hobie said they haven't made parts like that in years. He gave me the names of three people to write to—collectors—I did that last night. Maybe they'll have plugs and points they want to sell." Charlie tried to sound hopeful, but he wasn't.

If people collected something, why would they want to sell it? Particularly if things like that weren't made any more? He didn't mention his worry about the condenser. No sense in borrowing trouble. It was hard enough just keeping this whole thing secret, what with Hobie's questions, then having to smuggle the package past Mrs. Critch to avoid *her* curiosity. And then she had asked him questions anyway, making him think maybe she had caught a glimpse of the package through the window. Or maybe she just suspected something, what with him being late. Anyway, as she dished up dinner she had begun asking him about how much money his father had given him, and just what he'd done with it. Had Hobie told her he'd been in the hobby shop with a wad of bills? But Hobie wouldn't. At least Charlie hoped he wouldn't.

Rory opened the bag again and examined each item with care. He found the change wrapped in the sales slip and stuffed it into a tin can on the workbench.

"What are you going to do first?" Charlie asked. "Rig up those cogwheels for the needle valve?"

"No, sonny. I'm going to collect parts for a day or two and get the body work done. There'll be time while the glue's drying to take these rusted, infernal toys apart. By the time the prop gets here I ought to have the body repaired, the new cowling built, and the ailerons built and installed. And once we get that prop, sonny, we can find out how that engine runs! We'll just put the batteries in, pour in a little gas, flip that new prop, and give her a try!"

If she runs, Charlie thought. *If you can really bring*

it off, you crazy animal. He stared at the kangaroo rat, at the scattered gears and tools, and he thought that what Rory was trying to do was just wild.

It took ten days for the new prop to arrive. Charlie didn't see too much of the animals for a few days because the town had hit on a new scheme to get rid of the starlings, and Charlie, along with everyone else, had been staying up part of the night to turn the garden hose on the starlings to drive them off the roofs and make them so uncomfortable they would leave permanently. They didn't leave, of course, and at last the town had given up. Mrs. Critch had made him stay in bed in the daytime whether he could sleep or not, which he couldn't. When it was over, he was so gone for sleep that when the prop arrived he hardly remembered what should be in the package. Not until he opened it and found the prop did he come fully awake. He started right out to the dump with it, remembered that Rory would want some gas to try the engine, and swung back to dig a gas can out of his garage. He stopped at the Eagle Station to get the can filled, then went on to the dump.

Rory and Crispin were working away like crazy. Rory had mended the wing and repaired the hole in the fuselage. He had built a new cowling, too, which stood ready to cover the engine, and when Charlie arrived Rory was working on the rudder. He still had the ailerons to build and install. "And we're going to need a new windshield, sonny. Better get some plastic next time you're in the hobby shop. Can't find a thing out here that's fit to use."

"It's looking terrific, Rory."

"Well that's only the outside, sonny. Still have all the controls to rig. And the gas tank to put in. The flappin' tank should've been done first thing. You'd think there'd be plenty of cans the right size in the dump! The place is full of cans—cola cans, peanut cans, great big gallon cans—but not a flappin' thing the right size. Sure can't fly her with that dinky gas tank she's got now. We'd be landing to refuel every five minutes! You'd better ask in that hobby shop if they have a half-gallon tank, but I don't think they will. Sixteen ounces'll be about the biggest, I bet.

"We've fixed the cockpit seats so they come out and that section in between comes out. We're going to have to slip the tank in through the cockpits when we find it. Going to have to keep all the flappin' controls over to the side of the instrument panel, too, to get the tank past 'em. Flappin' nuisance!"

The body work had not been easy, Rory had had some trouble getting the hinges for the ailerons and rudder installed securely enough to suit him, and twice Crispin had glued his paws into the balsa ribs and had to be unstuck with hot water, making Rory cross at the delay. And then, of course, putting the paper smoothly over the balsa structure was a really touchy job. It had to be put on wet so it would shrink, and when it was wet it was delicate and hard to handle. It pulled and tore so easily that the two animals were in a terrible temper, shouting and snarling at each other before they got it smooth.

Now Charlie stood holding the can of gas and

the new prop as he watched Rory tear out cog-wheels from inside the cockpit and replace them with stronger ones from a toy derrick Crispin had found. "Flappin' clock's innards were too small," Rory growled. "I was afraid of that. But these babies'll do it, they'll control the fuel mixture just fine. Try 'er, sonny," he said as he tightened the last bolt.

Charlie reached into the cockpit and turned the handle for the fuel mixture as he watched the needle valve in the engine. Sure enough, the needle valve turned through the venturi tube smooth as silk.

He looked at Rory and winked.

"Still have to rig the throttle choke toggle switch," Rory said. "And get the controls brought in from the tail and the ailerons. But come on, sonny, let's get the prop on this baby and give her a whirl."

Charlie held one end of the prop, while Crispin lifted the other. Rory fitted the prop's hole over the engine shaft, put the nut on, and tightened it down. Then he got down from the cigar box he'd been standing on and fitted a funnel over the opening to the gas tank.

"Pour some of that gas in her, sonny." Charlie did, and Rory climbed into the front cockpit and nodded for Charlie to spin the prop. Charlie pulled the prop through slowly a few times, then spun it. Nothing happened. He spun it again and nothing. Again and again, and the engine didn't even cough.

Oh boy, Charlie thought. *What if she never runs! All that work on the plane and . . .*

Then on the tenth spin she coughed, caught,

63

coughed again . . . and died.

"Again!" Rory shouted. Charlie spun. She sputtered and died. They checked the action of the needle valve. "It's been a long time since she's run," Rory said.

The twelfth time Charlie spun her, she sputtered and held—she roared. Charlie reached behind the spinning prop and retarded the spark. Later Rory would be able to do that from the cockpit. Now she purred.

They grinned at each other through the windshield. But she purred like a pussycat with hiccups, Hic-*up*. Hic-*up*. Hic-*up*. They shook their heads. It was the points. She'd need new points, all right. But she was running. She was really running!

She sat shaking and rumbling, straining to be free, to loose herself from her tiedowns and lift into the sky. Rory was grinning from ear to ear.

Then she died completely, and when they tried to start her again, no luck. "Condenser," Rory growled at last. "Flappin' faulty condenser. They'll do that. Okay 'till they get warm, then, phlooey. Just our flappin' snakebit luck!"

"Oh, boy," Charlie said. He'd been afraid of this. "Hobie'll *never* have a condenser. I'll ask, though. Then I'll write to those people I wrote to about the spark plugs and the points. I haven't heard from one yet."

Charlie had thought Rory would be even more upset about the condenser than he was. Maybe he just wasn't letting on. The kangaroo rat stood looking at the plane with her new prop on, and his whiskers twitched into a big grin. "Don't she look fine, sonny! Say, you'll find that condenser, all right. You just write some more letters." Rory took up a wire brush and began to clean some cable. "Going to have to give her a name pretty soon. It don't seem right, keeping her nameless. Wish I knew what her real name was, what kind of plane she is. I'd guess this old biplane must have been built in the early twenties. Seems as if I've seen a picture like her somewhere—I've been wracking my brain trying to remember. Could have been any one of those old flying magazines at Turbine Field. Why, she might be the last one of her kind in the whole world."

"I could go over to the airfield and look in the flying magazines," Charlie said. "There're stacks of them over there. Her picture might be in one. They're all in my dad's office in the hangar, and I know where he keeps the key."

"Well say, sonny . . ."

"We could all go!" Crispin cried. "We could help you look, Charlie!"

Charlie considered. What harm could it do? "Okay," he said at last, "We'll do it. We'll go in the morning, first thing. There're probably some warm Cokes in the office. I'll bring the sandwiches."

CHAPTER

12

ON HIS way home Charlie stopped in the middle of town to watch old Mr. Trimble erect a scarecrow covered with shiny foil and bits of dangling tin. Charlie didn't think that would work on the starlings, but he didn't say anything.

Mr. Trimble saw him watching and looked sheepish. "I don't think this'll work, Charlie, but a fellow has to try something. I plan to hoist it up there under the streetlight where they flock at night, so the light'll shine on it. Have to try something," he repeated. "Say, you see this, Charlie?" Mr. Trimble hauled some worn, folded magazine pages out of his pocket. "Mrs. Strugg gave it to me. It tells all about starlings. It's from an old copy of *Sports Illustrated*." He unfolded the creased pages. "It even tells about a study made of them by the U.S. Department of Agriculture. Listen: 'It was generally believed—that birds do not go out of their way to browbeat other birds just for the pleasure of it. But that is what starlings did to bluebirds. Two bluebirds built their nest high on an elm tree in Norwalk, Connecticut, in spite of the raucous jeering of starlings gathered around watching them. The bluebirds finally left without nesting. A bird-watcher hurriedly built a birdhouse and the bluebirds returned and began putting nesting material in it. In their absence the starlings entered the birdhouse and threw out the nesting material. The bluebirds put it back. The starlings threw it out again. This went on for three days . . . finally the male bluebird was found dead beneath the birdhouse: the reasonable suspicion was that the starlings had something to do with its demise.' "

"My gosh," Charlie said. "And that was in a government report?"

"S'right here, Charlie." Mr. Trimble held out the magazine. "And look, here it says something about starling *invasion!* Skrimville isn't the only place this has happened. And it tells how they perched near the bluebirds and stared, wheezed and whistled."

"That's what they do, all right," Charlie said. He flicked a piece of dangling foil on the scarecrow. "Sure hope this thing works, Mr. Trimble."

"I don't know, Charlie. I really don't think it will. But a fellow has to try something, doesn't he?"

Charlie went on down Main Street, and as he passed the music store he saw Mush lurking in the shadows trying not to be seen and heard someone playing piano scales badly from the music store's lesson room. Charlie turned the corner, out of Mush's sight.

When he got home, there was a letter from his dad in the mailbox. Mrs. Critch was out shopping. With the house to himself, Charlie took his time making a triple decker sandwich, then he took it and his dad's letter to his room. It was not a very long letter, but it told him a good deal about the latest attempts to have the garbage dump closed and plowed under so the starlings would leave and the airfield could open again.

The county says it's up to the state to close the dump, his dad said. *And wouldn't you know, the state says it's up to the county. And the town won't do it because three other towns use that garbage dump and they* don't *want it plowed under. In other words,* his father said dryly, *It's the same old buck-passing we've been getting all along.* His dad had two or three harsher things to say about the state and county governments and ended by hoping that Charlie was getting along all right with Mrs. Critch and to call him if she got out of hand. Charlie grinned, tucked the letter into a safe place, and wrote a short note to his dad to tell him he was going to use the machine shop key to take a look at those old magazines.

He sure hoped that, if they plowed the garbage dump under, Rory would be finished with the plane. Even if the trash dump wasn't plowed up, there would be a lot of activity out there. He sat staring out the window, wishing he could snap his fingers and make the starlings disappear. He was so lost in thought he didn't realize he was looking at heavy rain clouds until he saw a platoon of starlings wheeling beneath the dark sky screaming angry defiance at it. They must be looking for shelter from the rain because it was too early for them to be roosting. This was only a small band, he couldn't see the rest. The first big drops began to fall, and Charlie wondered suddenly if the piano box roof would leak. He could imagine a drenched airplane and two soggy animals, wet beds and, worst of all, wet balsa wood and paper. He dropped his sandwich, raced to the garage through the beginning downpour, rooted among junk for the plastic drop cloths his dad used for painting, stuffed them in his jacket, and took off for the dump as the rain came down really hard. He saw Mrs. Critch's square bulk hurrying down the street toward him, loaded with bundles. He swerved his bike away as she yelled and pretended he didn't hear her. The rain poured down his collar, plastered his hair to his face, blurred his vision. He pedaled harder. He tried to remember how much stuff was piled on top the piano crate that might keep water off.

When he reached the dump, he found Rory and Crispin frantically pulling scraps of wrinkled tar paper up onto the roof of the piano crate. The rain had drenched everything on top the crate, and water was beginning to soak into the plywood. So far, it was dripping down inside the hangar in only one place, but soon it would be dozens. The two animals were half drowned, sputtering and shaking, with their fur plastered down so they looked naked. Charlie unrolled the plastic and pulled one end up over the top of the crate, covering kangaroo rat, lemming, and junk. He shouted directions as Rory and Crispin pulled and straightened the thin sheet, then crawled out. They anchored it with bits of metal, boards and some rods, then Charlie threw the second sheet over the first, and after a lot of wet scrabbling around they had a pretty secure roof. The animals dove for the hangar and Charlie collected some empty cans from the dump to put under leaks, then he crouched down inside the piano box next to the plane. Rory and Crispin sat huddled together on one of the cots. Thunder rolled, and lightning split the sky somewhere over near town.

Rory began to dry himself with a bit of paint-stained rag. Crispin unrolled a long red sock that must have been his pillow and wrapped it around his dripping shoulders.

"Them starlings made a real fuss when the rain started," Rory said. "Acted like they'd gone crazy, squawking and carrying on, wheeling and diving and throwing a regular tantrum. Maybe they thought they could drive the rain away."

"They were that way in town," Charlie said. "Looking for shelter, I guess. Not much shelter in the garbage dump."

Rory gave him a sour look and waved a paw at the mountains of trash. "Half of them are out there," he said shortly. "They pushed into every car body and turned-over tub they could find."

Charlie peered out but could see nothing but a sheet of rain. And now the wind began to shift and to drive rain into the hangar. He crawled outside and went to find something to shelter the door. He found a car hood leaning against some junk, then just as the rain let up, a big piece of plywood that was better. He wrestled this back toward the hangar as the sky turned a little brighter overhead. The rain had nearly ceased. But it was just a lull; heavier clouds were blowing in from the south. By the time he'd reached the hangar again, the wind had risen suddenly so it pushed and twisted at the plywood and hit him hard from behind; a sharp slamming wind—but it was more than wind that hit him! Bodies were hitting him. Hard, flying bodies. Beaks and claws struck him. He was knocked off balance by screaming starlings surging past him into the piano box. They boiled around him into the little hangar, thick as night, until the box was full of clawing birds, fighting for a perch, their voices rasping. Charlie could not see the two animals. He stared around frantically. Finally he glimpsed Rory leaping high among the mass of birds kicking for all he was worth; then the kangaroo rat disappeared. Charlie pushed in among the birds trying to feel fur, was nearly covered with thrashing feathers. He heard the thin paper on the plane tear under birds' claws, heard a strut crack. He swung his hand at the birds that covered the plane and drew his hand back bloodied. He reached back toward the cot where he had last seen the animals, and birds churned and exploded in his face. He heard Crispin cry out faintly. Birds were coming at him with open beaks. He saw Rory leap again and grabbed at him wildly, missed him, grabbed again and felt the kangaroo rat snatch at his fingers. They got hold of each other

somehow among feathers and claws, and Charlie lifted Rory out, trying to protect him from the striking birds.

"Crispin's down there!" Rory cried.

Charlie shoved Rory inside his jacket and reached toward the cots, with birds pecking him so sharply they brought tears. He tipped over a cot in his haste, shook off a bird that would not let go—then, at last, he felt the furry little lemming lying beneath the table, quite still.

He cupped the lemming in both hands and lifted him out, then backed away from the hangar and knelt with rain pouring down his neck. Crispin lay very still in his bloodied hands. He bent to listen for a heartbeat but could hear none. He pushed the lemming inside his jacket with Rory as birds flew out at him. He slapped at attacking birds and felt the two animals stirring against his stomach. At last he was able to open his jacket. "Is Crispin all right? Is he alive?"

"He's okay, sonny. I think he just fainted." Rory was bleeding badly.

"Well, hang on tight; I'm going to get rid of those birds!" Charlie dug into the nearest trash heap until he found a good-sized piece of lumber, then knelt once more before the hangar and began to flail right and left, taking care not to hit the plane. He sent birds squawking and flying at him with rage. He had to pull his collar over his face against the storm of beating wings. At last he felt wings begin to brush by him as birds leaped away—but others battled on, heads thrust forward, open beaks hissing, wings spread. The biplane looked terrible. Some flaps of paper hung down, a rib showed. She was so covered with bird droppings he could only guess at the damage. The cots had collapsed and so had the table, and tools were scattered everywhere among droppings and dark feathers and dead birds. Charlie poked with the two-by-four at the remaining clutch of birds so they screamed at him with fury, but finally rose into the rain, their eyes never leaving him. "Go on!" he yelled. "Get out of here!" They circled him threateningly. He swung the two-by-four, and at last they flew away.

And then Charlie heard, down inside his jacket where the two wet bodies wriggled against his stomach, Crispin's little voice saying, "Move over, Rory! There's a button in my ribs!"

Charlie opened his jacket. The kangaroo rat jumped to his shoulder and stood scowling at the damaged plane. He was soaking wet and bloody. His paws were clenched, and his eyes were dark with anger. The lemming crept out too, and when he saw the mess, he began to chitter with terrible fury, his teeth going like triphammers and his eyes flashing. They all stared at the sorry, sorry plane. "Bird brains!" Rory said. "Mindless, no good bird brains. When the Good Lord made the world, he sure didn't have to make starlings!" He turned and spat. "It was dark as sin under them flappin' birds, I thought sure

75

our number was up! And I bet I've got their stinkin' lice all over me!" He glared at Crispin, who was still chittering. "Well what're we waiting for, sonny! Let's get this mess cleaned up. Let's get that plane washed and see what kind of shape she's in!"

13

THE cloud-heavy sky darkened into night before they had scrubbed the plane clean. They worked by the light from Charlie's bike lamp, which picked out harshly the jagged rents in the plane: five long tears where paper had been pulled away from ribs, many rips from sharp claws, two broken ribs. Charlie found some rusty nails and a rock, and they rolled the plane inside and nailed the plywood over the hangar to keep the birds out, leaving a crack so the animals could come and go. "I'll bring out a flashlight," Charlie said, "so you can work in there. It's going to be dark as pitch even in the daytime."

"Afraid you're right, sonny. I hate working shut in like that, but I guess it can't be helped." Then, seeing the lemming's expression as he stared at the hurt plane, "Why, we'll fix her up good as new! What's been done once, youngster, can sure be done again!"

There were no stars, no moon, the clouds must still be thick overhead. As Charlie started home through the pitch black dump, he wondered if Mrs. Critch was waiting up to yell at him for missing dinner. The light from his bike lamp reflected in the puddles and glanced off wet trash, and his tires sloshed through deep water and skidded in the mud. His clothes and shoes were soaking and cold. His stomach rumbled with hunger, and he wondered if she'd try to make him go to bed without dinner. He wished he had the sandwich he'd left on the desk. He pedaled on through the wet night and was pretty glad when he hit pavement at last, and gladder still when he saw the lights of home, even if Mrs. Critch *was* waiting up for him. He could see her dark, square shape silhouetted against the shade. She'd make some kind of scene, you could bet on it. He wiped his feet, then dripped into the living room soggy and cold and grim.

She had made herself very comfortable in his dad's chair and was watching the ten o'clock news. She looked up and smiled. "Have you had your dinner, Charlie? There's spaghetti in the oven keeping warm," she said pleasantly. "And salad and apple pie. I'll just dish it up for you, then go on to bed."

He couldn't say anything. Why wasn't she giving him holy heck? He went to his room, got out of his wet clothes and into his pajamas, then settled himself alone before a huge plate of spaghetti. When he finished eating, he made some peanut butter sandwiches for their trip to the airfield the next day, then went to bed still wondering what was wrong with Mrs. Critch.

When he rose the next morning to find his favorite breakfast on the table and still not a word of reprimand, he grew uneasy. He wolfed his breakfast, slipped some pancakes and bacon into his napkin, hid this with the sandwiches in his jacket, and left.

He found the two animals working by the light of a candle stub inside the boarded-up hangar. He had brought a flashlight and some extra batteries. He shone the light in on the plane and saw that they had already repaired the tears and were working on a broken strut. The new unpainted paper shone thin and transluscent in the flashlight beam. Charlie unwrapped the pancakes and bacon, somewhat stuck to the paper napkin, and the animals ate it all with great relish, including the syrupy paper.

When they started for the airfield, Rory, whose beak-wounds were beginning to stiffen and hurt, rode on Charlie's shoulder. Crispin, his stomach full of breakfast, went to sleep in Charlie's pocket.

The mechanic's hangar was an immense building. Beside the big hangar door was a small door into Charlie's father's office. Charlie unlocked this and opened a second door between office and hangar so the animals could see the planes. Crispin stood staring in awe, and even Rory seemed impressed. The roof of the hangar must seem terribly high to the lemming, but of course Rory had spent the winter in the hangar at Turbine Field so it was nothing new to him. He admired the six planes stored there, though. Charlie opened a closet in the office and began to haul out magazines, years' and years' accumulation of flying magazines. He piled them on the floor around the desk, and they all began to turn pages, looking for a picture of an old biplane with a pointed nose.

After what seemed hours of turning dusty pages, Charlie began to yawn. Crispin had gone to sleep. At midmorning Rory woke the lemming, and they split a warm Coke three ways into yellowed paper cups. Then Rory went into the big hangar to look at the planes again and discovered a puddle of water in the far corner and a small hole high above in the tin roof. "Looks like the roofing tin's been blown back, sonny. See there, where that piece is all bright instead of rusty. That patch must've been covered before. Hole's not much bigger than a pencil, but there sure was a lot of rain came in."

Charlie found a bucket, emptied the gears and bolts out of it, and placed it to catch any further leaks.

"That's a nice Cessna 180," Rory said. "You'd think these fellows wouldn't just let their planes sit here, that they'd be out flying in spite of the blasted birds."

"They did until that jet crashed. Then everyone— well, they're not flying any more," Charlie said.

"Seems to me a whole flappin' town full of humans ought to be smart enough to get rid of them *somehow!*"

"Well they . . ." Charlie began, when a faint voice spoke from somewhere in the shadows. Charlie caught his breath, and they all stared toward the far corner.

"It's harder," came the voice. "It's harder to drive off starlings than you might think." The voice came from the crowded shelves, but they could see no one. It had been a very faint voice. Crispin stood on his hind legs, peering up at the clutter of engine parts and tools.

"There!" Rory said, pointing. Three shelves up, between some oil cans, they could now see a huddle of bright feathers, brown and red and white.

"Come on out of there!" Rory commanded.

A big bird stepped forward. He had a white breast spotted with brown, bright red triangles on his cheeks, and a black apron beneath his throat like a wide collar. He looked at them for a long time and seemed to consider Charlie particularly. There was an air of grandeur about him, but one of suffering, too. At last he spoke again. "Please, have you something to eat? I am nearly starved." He said this with quiet dignity. "It has been two days since I've eaten and . . ."

Charlie rushed for the office, brought back the lunch, and began tearing off pieces of sandwich.

The big bird ate carefully, though they could tell he wanted to gulp the food. He fluttered down once to drink from the puddle, then settled on the floor near Rory and Crispin. He was taller than they, and larger than a starling. They could see he had been nearly starved, yet he conducted himself with courtesy. They did not ask him questions until he had eaten his fill, drunk twice more, and seemed stronger.

Charlie had no idea what kind of bird he was, though he thought he had seen some like him. He was certainly handsome with his spotted chest, striped back and wings, and the red slashes on his cheeks. His eyes, dark and kind, did not have the beady glimmer of a starling's eyes. Nor was his voice like a starling's, but soft and calm. "He's a flicker," Crispin whispered to Charlie. "A red-shafted flicker. I met one in Canada, Charlie!"

"How did you get in?" Charlie asked. "Were you in here when we locked the doors? But that was six week ago!"

"Oh no, I wasn't here then or I would be dead by now," the flicker said. "I came in through that hole in the roof five days ago. It was a bigger hole when I first found it. But let me explain. I was trying to find a new home. We were desperate. We were living—are still living, I hope—in a hole in the wall on the outside of this building. But the starlings came." His voice faltered, and it was a minute before he could go on.

At last he said, "I have to get out, I have to find my family. I left my wife and three children to try to find a safe place. The starlings were making life unbearable for us. We were so afraid for the children. I knew about the hole on the roof, and I came up to investigate. I was perched there, looking in, trying to see if there was a way to get out once I got in, when the rusted roof gave way under me. Somehow I got tangled in the roof itself and was through and in the air before I could claw my way back. And in my struggle I must have dislodged part of the roof—one of those tin sheets—so it nearly covered the hole. Later, I couldn't budge it. Nor could my wife; she tried from outside. She dropped worms and grubs down to me for a while. But now—now it has been

nearly two days since I've seen her. It was hard on her, I know, feeding those three hungry children all alone, and feeding me as well. I know she's exhausted, and she . . . I'm very worried about her, about all of them. My children were nearly ready to fly."

Rory had sat quiet through the flicker's story, but now he burst out, "Flappin' no good starlings!" And his whiskers were taut with fury. "Get up there on the boy's shoulder, friend! Give him a hand up, Charlie! We'll just see about that family of yours!" He leaped to Charlie's shoulder in one bound and balanced himself adroitly as Charlie knelt to lift the flicker, then lift Crispin.

Charlie made his way out through the small side door of the office and around the building as the flicker directed. "There! There it is," the flicker cried, and he took off so suddenly he nearly blew Crispin away with the wind of his wings. The bird flew straight up the side of the building to disappear in a hole in the wood siding.

He was gone for some minutes. When he returned he looked very lost. "I think the children must have flown—I pray they did, I pray they got away safely. The nest is cold. There has been no one in it for some time."

They searched the ground for bodies but found none. So at last they went back into the hangar. The flicker rested a bit longer, ate once more, then prepared to go in search of his family. While he rested, he told them how the starlings had discovered his nest when the children were only half-grown and defense-

84

less, and how the dark birds had tried to push the babies out so they would fall to the ground and be killed. The starlings had attacked both himself and his wife as well. The two had fought back, of course, but it had not been easy to fight two dozen starlings, gather food, and guard their helpless young. So the old flicker had gone in search of a safer place. "But then I fell in the hole. It was a stupid thing to do, and I made everything worse, and now they may all be dead. And if they *did* get away, there are few enough places to go with the town overrun and no other trees but the pine grove. The starlings are apt to go back there at any time. I'm sure there isn't a decent bird left in the town, with starlings roosting there."

"Would it take your children long to learn to fly?" Crispin asked. The lemming was quite in awe of the flicker.

"Oh, no. Once they're ready, their wings strong enough, it's just a matter of that first surge off the nest. They won't fall, you see, once their wings can hold them; they're out there on the wind suddenly, excited and scared, and they just start flapping for all they're worth. It's harder to get back, to make their wings pull them up. But they do it." The flicker sat still, seeming to remember other families, other times. And the three friends sat before him in silence, each thinking his own thoughts.

———————

THEY watched the flicker depart, rising into the wind in an undulating flight as if he rode ocean waves. A lilting but purposeful flight. When they returned to the magazines, the dusty pages of *Pilot* and *Flying* seemed tedious indeed, for the flicker had awakened in each of them a strange longing and restlessness.

"Well," Rory said. "Well, we don't *have* to go poking in them magazines."

"We do if you want her to have her own name," Charlie said absently, gazing off in the direction the flicker had taken. He hoped he found his family out there.

"Old magazines make me sneeze," Crispin said and promply went to sleep under the desk. Charlie and Rory looked at each other, shook their heads, and settled down half-heartedly to turn pages.

There were plenty of old planes, biplanes, tri-wings, homemade jobs. Tiger Moths and Sopwith Pups and old Fairchilds. But nothing at all that looked like Rory's plane, with her sharp-pointed nose and rakish air. And the old magazines surely did make them sneeze. They had almost given up when, several hours later, Rory turned a page, stared, and let out a whoop of surprise that made Charlie jump. *"Fox!"* he shouted. *"Fox! She's a Fox! Look there! There she is!"*

Crispin ran onto the page still half-asleep. "Where, Rory? Where?" And no one could see anything with the lemming milling around. Charlie lifted him off, and there was her picture all right, her pointed nose, her four wings and twin cockpits. *"The Fairey Fox Bomber,"* Charlie read. *"Designed by Charles Fairey in 1924.* Wow, a bomber!"

"Fairy Fox?" said Crispin.

"That's the name of the man who designed her, sonny. Fairey's *his* name. We don't have to call her the Fairey Fox. Her name'll be *Fox.* Painted in big red letters on her fuselage."

"She looks like a fox, Rory, with her pointed nose. I saw a fox once outside our snow tunnel, but Mama pulled me back in right away."

"She sure *does* look like a fox." Rory grinned, aimed a kick at the untidy stack of magazines, and did a double flip in the air. He felt great. It was just the right name for her. A sleek, quick fox of a plane. "Come on, you two, let's get back to our own hangar. We have work to do. And bring those flight and weather manuals there on the shelf, Charlie Gribble. I'll have to have a little ground school if I'm going to fly the *Fox* high and handsome."

The minute he was back in his own hangar, Rory found a pencil and began to letter FOX carefully on the fuselage; and by the time Charlie returned the next morning, the letters FOX shone bright red on each side.

Rory had painted all her repairs, too. You couldn't tell she'd ever been hurt. She looked sharp indeed. The sun glanced off her cracked windshield and her clean, new paint. And now that she had a name, she seemed really to come alive, seemed almost as eager as Rory and Crispin to be off and flying. She and Rory and Crispin were three companions now, poised on the brink of an adventure no creatures had ever attempted. An adventure Charlie could never share. He would have given anything at that moment to be as small as the two animals, to be able to crowd into the *Fox's* cockpit beside Rory and take off to see the world.

"The next thing, sonny, is the gas tank," Rory said, "and that flappin' condenser. Gas tank should've been the first thing to go in, not the last!" the kangaroo rat grumbled. "A million cans out there! Lard cans, cat food cans—and every flappin' one of 'em either too big or too small or the wrong shape! It's been twice as much work, not having the tank. If we don't find a gas tank pretty soon, we might as well forget about seeing the flappin' world!"

Charlie couldn't blame Rory; he couldn't fly the Fox without gas. The old tank, which Rory had torn out, would hardly have been enough to get her across Skrimville.

"And what about the condenser, Sonny? Did you

write to those people?"

"I wrote. But I haven't even had answers to my first letters. Maybe no one is going to answer, maybe . . ."

But Rory had picked up a scrap of paper bag and was standing at the work table scribbling figures. "The *Fox* ought to weigh in at about eight pounds, including fuel. Then, plus baggage and Crispin and me, say nine pounds. We're going to need a scale, sonny."

"I'll bring our bathroom scale."

"Nine pounds," the kangaroo rat repeated. "And she ought to fly about fifty miles an hour, give or take accounting for the wind. At that weight, I'd say she'd get about a mile and a half per ounce. Let's see, that would be—thirty-two ounces to a quart—that's forty-eight miles to a quart of gas. She won't carry a half-gallon like I thought at first. Let's see, that's, um, four quarts to the gallon . . ." Rory scribbled on. "That would be one-hundred-ninety-two miles to the gallon, sonny! Pretty good for an old gas burner! We have to find a long, thin quart can that'll fit in the fuselage. A quart'll give us just about an hour's flying time between refills, and almost fifty miles distance. Going to have to stay close to farm country, though. Best place to get gas and oil will be from farm tanks. Of course we could siphon the gas out of cars and leave some money on the hood, but that doesn't give us the oil we need to mix in. And anyway I don't like coming down in towns. I'd rather be out in the country, no matter how you look at it.

Rory had been watching the dump carefully for a gas tank, going out every day to scrounge. He had set aside several cans that could be rebuilt if nothing else turned up. "I hate like heck to rebuild one. My seams won't be as good as machine made, and it's a flappin' lot of unnecessary work!"

It was nearly a week later, and still no gas tank, when the spark plugs and points arrived. Skrimville was involved in another wild scheme to get rid of the starlings that involved glue on all the utility wires, and Charlie was glad to get out of town before someone handed him a gluepot and pointed him toward a ladder. He scorched out to the dump on his bike, batted away at some starlings that were flying around his head, and found Rory scrounging in some new trash for useful parts. He handed Rory the package and the letter that had come with it. There were four new spark plugs and the two new sets of points. The package had come from Mary Starr Colver. Charlie guessed the second letter he had written to her, about the condenser, had crossed her letter, because she didn't seem to have gotten it. But she had answered his question anyway, almost as if she had known they might need a condenser. Her letter said,

Dear Charlie Gribble,

I'm sending you the parts you're looking for. The cost is itemized at the bottom of the letter. I agree, it's hard to find parts for antique planes in a small

town—or in any town, for that matter. So I am sending you some information on the Antique Model Club, and some ads from their magazine. One small manufacturer still makes these spark plugs. The magazine has a want ad column, too, and we get parts from each other as well as from the ads. If you are rejuvenating an old plane that has had a good deal of use and been out in the weather as you said, there's a chance your condenser will be faulty. Harry Jones Company, in Millville, Oregon, makes condensers, and you can write to them for one and send a money order. I'm enclosing their ad, too, with the prices.

Good luck to you. I would like to hear more about your project. I hope your old biplane—whatever she turns out to be—gives you a lot of good flying.

Your friend,
Mary Starr Colver.

That afternoon Charlie, stopping at Hobie's Hobby Shop for some solder and another wrench for Rory, stared at the shelves in front of him and let out a yelp. "*Oh boy! How dumb can you get! I never even thought to look in here!*"

"Look for what, Charlie?" Hobie was down under the counter getting the wrench.

"Right in front of my nose! I'll bet anything it's the right size!"

Hobie rose from behind the counter and followed Charlie's gaze. "What're you looking at, Charlie? Them turpentine cans? They've been sitting on that shelf in that same spot for two years."

91

"Could I see that one a minute, Hobie?"

Hobie handed him the can.

He measured it with his finger. With the length of his hand. "I think it's right. I *think* so."

"What d' you need it for Charlie?"

"Gas tank. Remember, we looked and you can't get any over sixteen ounces."

"What're you going to do, fly that thing around the world?"

Charlie stared at Hobie. "Maybe," he said. "Can I take it Hobie, and if it isn't right bring it back?"

"Long as you don't use up the turpentine."

When Rory saw the can, he let out a war whoop, got the ruler, measured the can, then scowled up at Charlie. "You mean to tell me the flappin' thing was there all the time! That you *saw* it there, and you . . ."

Charlie hung his head. "I thought you could find a can. And then when you couldn't, and you asked me to buy one and Hobie said he couldn't get any that big I was in a hurry and . . . and I'm sorry, Rory. I'll bet I've seen that can a thousand times and I never even—*oh nuts!*"

"It's okay, sonny," the kangaroo rat said, "We've got it now. This here's going to make a super gas tank! Come on, sonny, you take it over the other side of the dump and empty the turpentine out where it won't stink the whole place up. We'll rinse it out good, cut a hole for the gas line—Did you get that solder I asked for?"

"Yeah. But why so much?"

"I was about ready to cut up one of those other cans and *build* a flappin' tank, sonny."

While Charlie went to empty the turpentine can, Rory dug out a connection from the heap of parts he had accumulated and found a length of gas line. Then he built up a hot fire in the hubcap and laid half a dozen nails around it with their points well into the embers. By the time he and Charlie got the hole cut, the nails were hot enough to solder with.

Holding a nail wrapped in rag, Rory flowed melted solder into the seams as Charlie watched. When he was finished soldering, they tested the tank for leaks by filling it with water. Then they drained it well and laid it near the fire until it was quite dry inside, fixed the three leaks, filled it with water again, emptied and dried it again, and finally were ready to install it.

And that was the hardest job, getting the tank into the front section of the fuselage. Rory removed the seats from the cockpits and the support between the cockpits, but even then the tank was a tight fit. At last, though, it was secure. They got the gas lines hooked up. They replaced the support and the seats —and Crispin began to fuss. "What if the gas explodes, Rory? What will we do then?"

"If that tank explodes, sonny, there won't be enough left of either one of us to worry about it."

That seemed to settle the lemming. At least it shut him up. But he must have gotten out on the wrong side of the bed that morning because soon he began to complain about the rear cockpit not having any controls to fly the plane. "I'll just be a passenger! What if something happens to you, Rory? What if you get sick? You'll have all the controls, and I won't be able to reach them. We could crash, Rory, and I wouldn't be able to . . ."

"You would take off your seat harness, sonny, climb over the fuselage to the front cockpit, reach around me, and fly her! Just see if you wouldn't! Just like an old stunt flier. Like one of them wing walkers." Rory grinned, but Crispin was so disappointed that he could not fly the *Fox* that he began to chitter and would pay no attention to Rory.

"There ain't enough room to run cables from the controls back to the second cockpit, sonny! I had enough trouble rigging them for one. With all the cogs and gears and levers, a second set of gears might foul up the first and—well there'd be no end to the complications."

Charlie picked the lemming up to try to cheer him, but Crispin scowled with such fury that Charlie thought he would bite. It had been a long time since Crispin had laid a tooth on him. "Oh, *come* on, Crispin! I'd like to fly her too. Don't you think *I'd* like to climb in the *Fox* and take off with you? I'll be left behind all alone!"

That made Crispin stop glaring, but he refused to say anything to comfort Charlie and was still sulking when Charlie left late in the afternoon.

The lemming would have sulked until bedtime if the starlings had not begun to gather around the hangar early in the summer evening just as the day

began to turn cool. The dark birds lined up on refrigerators and bedsprings and tires and stared silently down on the closed hangar, and some crowded
right up to the plywood and stared in through the
crack. Rory glared out at them. He'd like to lob a
rock at those beady eyes, but he guessed a rock
chucked at that bunch would only rile them into
another wild attack. What the flappin' heck did they
want? What fascinated them so? They hung around
until roosting time, then flew off.

"Why did they do that, Rory?"

"I don't know, sonny. Maybe they're bored with
life. They've got no more birds to bedevil—they've
driven all the decent birds away—so now they're
picking on us. You know, sonny, boredom is a sign
of an empty mind. And those birds have the emptiest
minds going."

15

THE birds were back the next morning, two dozen of them perched on the trash hills when Rory and Crispin awoke. They hung around until noon, coming in shifts of sometimes two or three, sometimes so many they made a solid black line along the horizon of trash. And as they waddled up to the plywood to peer in, their bow-legged, swinging walk was ugly and insolent. They flew off when Charlie arrived.

"What do they want?" Charlie said, staring after them. "What were they hanging around for?"

"Something in their dim minds makes 'em like to bother folks, sonny. I suppose they can't help it," Rory said irritably. Charlie guessed Rory had had about all the starlings he could take.

But as annoying as the starlings were, they forgot them completely the day the condenser arrived.

Charlie had written off to the Harry Jones Company to order it the day they received the letter and package from Mary Starr Colver. He had sent a money order for the condenser, and then had written to Miss Colver, too, and sent her a money order for the points and plugs and thanked her for them. He had told her that the biplane had turned out to be a 1924 Fairey Fox. He'd told her how the plane was coming on; and when he spoke of working on the plane, he said "we," but of course he didn't tell her who "we" meant. He had thanked her for the information about the condenser manufacturer and the Antique Model Club, and said he hoped the *Fox* would be flying soon.

Now, with the condenser finally there, the *Fox* was nearly ready to fly. "The new points are in, sonny. The gas lines're attached. The gas tank's full. The controls work smooth as silk, and the new windshield went in real good. She's almost ready, this baby's almost ready to take on the world! Why, if it hadn't been for you, sonny, I'd not be nearly so far along. Why, I'd have been until Christmas getting her in shape."

The leather upholstery cut from a wrecked car was soft and smooth on the seats. The seat harnesses were snug and secure. The little plane had had a coat of wax over her paint, and when Charlie removed the plywood from the hangar, she seemed to be waiting impatiently to be off.

When finally Rory tightened the last bolt on the condenser and fixed the cowling over the engine, the three stared at each other with wonder. The *Fox* was really complete. A real, honest-to-goodness flying machine! Rory climbed into the front cockpit and nodded to Charlie.

Charlie spun the prop.

She caught. She died. She caught again and purred. She purred smooth as silk; she ran like a dream, like a brand-new engine—better than new. She strained to be free of Charlie's grasp, tugging eagerly toward the sky. There was a tear of joy in Rory's eye as he killed the engine and climbed down from the cockpit. "Come on, you two, let's get this baby out on the runway."

Charlie hesitated. A row of starlings was staring down at them from atop radiators and refrigerators and old tires, their purple sheen catching the sun. Rory followed his gaze.

"Hang the starlings, sonny! Grab a handful of rocks and come on!" The kangaroo rat began to push the Fox down the path, and Crispin ran to help.

"Well," Charlie said, "at least I can carry her." He picked up the *Fox* and, with the kangaroo rat and the lemming walking in front, headed for the airstrip. It would be wiser to wait—but wait for what? The starlings might be there forever. And he knew how Rory felt, that it was impossible for the kangaroo rat to wait one flappin' minute to get the *Fox* in the air.

When they reached the strip, he set the *Fox* down on the asphalt; she looked very small there. The lemming and the kangaroo rat looked even smaller.

"Okay, sonny, I'm going to learn just the way I told you the first pilots learned. I'm going to weight her down until I get used to the controls. Then I'll take some of the weight out, so I can learn to take off and land.

They loaded the *Fox* with stones, and Rory climbed into the front cockpit. This time Crispin spun the prop. Charlie held his breath as the lemming gave a mighty spin, another, and ducked away just as the prop took hold. The engine roared, then settled into a sweet purr as Rory retarded the spark. Charlie got a good grip on a rock, just in case. Rory tightened his seat harness and began to taxi down the strip. Charlie watched with apprehension, Crispin watched eagerly, and the starlings came flying low overhead and landed at the edge of the airstrip.

Rory was pretty excited. He taxied to the end of the strip, turned, and taxied back. He worked the ailerons and the elevators and the rudder to get used to each. He felt the *Fox* strain to lift herself; but the rocks held her earthbound.

When at last he threw out half the rocks, the *Fox* was able to lift into the wind—but not very high. She pulled upward only to be forced down with the weight. He was busy then, trying to bring her down as smoothly as he could. The first few landings were bumpy, which annoyed him considerably.

At last his landings smoothed out and became more coordinated. His takeoffs smoothed. He was getting the feel of the controls, of turning and directing the wind. When finally he taxied her to the side of the strip to dump the rest of the stones, he felt good. And a little nervous. He tossed out the rocks, twitched his whiskers, and sent the *Fox* down the runway into the wind for a full takeoff. He gave her power and right rudder, eased back on the stick—

and she leaped skyward. She flew up into the wind as nice as any plane ever had.

She was flying! Really flying! She lifted, bouyed by the wind.

And at once she was surrounded by starlings pushing close to her wings, crowding her tail. Rory's blood went cold. If they wrecked this plane, he'd kill every one of them.

Below he could see Charlie running out onto the field waving his arms, trying to drive them away. But he knew Charlie wouldn't throw a rock and risk hitting the *Fox*, and there was no other way Charlie could help him. Rory banked without thinking how he knew what to do, and put her in a steep dive that he must have learned from the books because, if he had thought about it first, he wouldn't have tried it. He pulled her out close to the ground and near to Charlie, giving Charlie a perfect shot at the starlings that flew thick on his tail. He saw Charlie raise his arm and let fly, saw the starlings behind him explode, screaming. But they regrouped again at once and were all over the *Fox*, wings in his face, feathers flying. Starlings dove at him face to face, beaks open.

Rory stared at them and suddenly he was too mad to think. He swung the *Fox* around and dove her straight at the birds. They paused in midair, hissing a long scream. They were not agile fliers, and the *Fox* was right on top of them. They broke away left and right, and Rory knew if she hit them she would go down—knew he was acting foolishly, but was too mad to stop.

He glimpsed Charlie staring up, shouting something, but the words were lost. Rory dove at the flock again, and they fled in all directions. The prop had nearly touched them—but the *Fox* continued to purr. Luck. Pure blind luck. The air was full of feathers, but the little *Fox* flew evenly through them. The flock hung below for some time, keeping its distance, the birds whistling to each other as if in conference. Rory was about to land while he had the chance when suddenly they clustered again and swung—not toward the *Fox* but toward Charlie so fast he could only duck sideways. They swept low over Charlie and snatched up the helpless lemming. They had Crispin aloft, dangling between two of them. Rory felt sick. He could see Charlie leaping and shouting. A starling dropped Crispin from a terrible height. He fell, twisting. Another starling caught him. The little ball of fur was dropped again, snatched out of the air, and hung limply from the beak of a third starling.

They tossed the lemming higher and higher, flipping him back and forth like a limp ball.

Rory circled. There was nothing he could do without hurting Crispin, nothing Charlie could do. He heard the lemming scream, a thin, terrified voice in the sky.

Then Rory saw something sweep fast through the sky, a strong, undulating flight that overtook the starlings and plowed into their midst. They exploded in every direction as the flicker's beak jabbed at them. The old flicker caught the lemming in midair, wheeled, and dove down with starlings close on his tail. Rory swung the *Fox* around and took off after the starlings. When he glanced back, the flicker had made it to Charlie, was perched on Charlie's arm with the lemming safe beside him. Then the flicker leaped into the sky, again after the starlings, jabbing cruelly with his long beak. Rory dove. Between Rory's dives and the flicker, the birds soon abandoned the chase and headed back toward the garbage dump.

Rory landed the *Fox* feeling shaky and weak.

Charlie was kneeling in the middle of the runway holding the lemming in his hands. The little creature lay very still. Rory and the flicker stood staring as Charlie tried to feel a heartbeat and could not. The flicker hopped onto Charlie's arm and cocked his head next to the lemming's chest. He listened, then looked up at Charlie. "He is alive. His heart is beating very fast and very faintly. It is shock. You must keep him warm in your hands until he comes around. Shock, and fear. Keep him very warm."

CHAPTER

16

———

THEY returned to the hangar, and while Rory wiped some oil spatters from the belly of the *Fox*, Charlie sat in the sun holding the lemming in his cupped hands to keep him warm. Crispin did not move. The flicker, having returned with them, waited silently beside Charlie for the little animal to revive. Charlie chafed the lemming's paws and kept his head lower than his feet, which he remembered you should do from reading a first aid book. He could remember nothing else that had to do with shock, only some information about tourniquets and snakebite that didn't apply at all.

Crispin had bled from several wounds, and they washed them. Rory said it was only the skin that was cut. The lemming's skin was very loose, it pulled away easily from his body like a loose coat, and the starlings' beaks had pierced only that loose skin. But even though he had only surface wounds he slept on.

As Charlie held Crispin, he looked at the flicker waiting there so concerned, and he wanted to ask the big bird about his family. But if he had found them, wouldn't they be with him now? And if he had not, such a question would be painful.

But Rory was not one to let things lie. He studied the flicker, and finally he said, "No luck yet?" The flicker shook his head.

They were silent. The sun shone down. The rust and new grass sparkled in the summer brightness, but the three were wrapped in gloom at the loss of the flicker's family and at the thought that the lemming might never wake again.

Life seemed to Charlie without purpose when such things could happen.

Life seemed to Rory diabolical in its twistings, a puzzle. He wished he had somehow protected the lemming from those starlings.

And then suddenly, the lemming stirred. He took hold of Charlie's thumb and pulled himself up. He stared around him vaguely. He looked at Charlie. He stared down at Rory and at the flicker. And his expression was blank. He recognized none of them.

The flicker departed at last, saddened by Crispin's condition, but committed to the search for his family. Rory and Charlie stared at the confused lemming until Rory, able to stand it no longer, went off toward the center of the dump.

The lemming curled up in a tight little ball and closed his eyes, as if there was nothing in the world he cared to look at. Charlie put him on his cot and covered him with his blue blanket, then practiced lobbing rocks at a tin can and wished it were a starling. Pretty soon Rory came back dragging a small transistor radio he had spotted some time before. "If you could get batteries for this thing, sonny, maybe it would cheer the little fellow. And cheer me, too. I've got used to his chatter, I guess. I don't think I can stand this silence."

Charlie took the batteries out of his bike light. They fit, but the radio wouldn't play. "No one would throw it away if it could play," he grumbled irritably. "Besides, how can you think about a radio when—when . . ."

"Sonny, with a small sick kangaroo rat or a puppy, you need something talking and comfortable to make them feel secure. Maybe it's the same with a hurt lemming. Now try the connections and see if they're loose!"

Charlie bent the copper connections, slipped the batteries back in, and turned the switch. The radio bleated. He turned it down and set it near the lemming, who seemed only vaguely aware of it.

Rory swept out the hangar, dusted off the plane, and made some minor adjustments to the engine. The radio played rock, and then the news came on. Charlie found a Hershey bar in his pocket, and he and Rory shared it. When they offered a little bit to Crispin, he looked appalled at the smell and turned his head away. Charlie and Rory discussed what to do for him, but could think of nothing helpful. Then they turned to thinking up schemes to get rid of the starlings, but nothing seemed good enough to try. There was not a starling to be seen this afternoon, as if they had satisfied their hunger for making folks miserable, at least for a little while. The radio played softly, and finally the lemming snuggled up to it.

Late in the afternoon Charlie and Rory nailed the plywood over the hangar, left a crack for the door, and went out to the dump to scrounge, just for something to do. The lemming was still sleeping.

Charlie found a toy saucepan that would be useful on the trip, and Rory discovered a bit of fleece that would make a warm coat for the youngster. "Get's cold flying," he muttered, and they both thought the same thing. *Would* the youngster be flying? Or would he just continue to lie on his bunk and not know them?

"Maybe—maybe a doctor or a veterinarian—" Charlie began.

"There ain't no bones broken, sonny, but maybe . . ."

And at that moment they heard Crispin shout and looked up to see the youngster running toward them. "Rory! Charlie!" The youngster knew their names! But *what* was he shouting?

"Mary Starr Colver! Mary Starr Colver!"

Charlie and Rory stared at each other, puzzled. Had the youngster slipped a cog? Why would he be shouting the name of the lady who had sent the spark plugs? The lemming scorched to a stop in front of Rory. "Mary Starr Colver, she was on the news," he squeaked, almost too excited to talk.

"Mary Starr Colver?" Charlie said. "Why would she . . ."

"It said," Crispin panted, " 'Our salute for today

to—to Mary Starr Colver' and—oh, something about her being the foremost woman in American avi—avi . . ."

"*Aviation?*" Rory and Charlie both said together.

"Yes. And about how she's won air races in her own plane, and about how courageous she was after it happened."

"After *what* happened, sonny?"

"*I* don't know. A commercial for soap flakes came on."

Charlie and Rory stared at the lemming.

Finally Rory said, "We've been writing to a woman pilot! Well how about that!"

"So that's why she's interested in model planes," Charlie said. "But if she's a pilot, for Pete's sake, why does she bother with models?"

"*I* don't know, Charlie, but she was on the news and she's famous." The little animal looked as bright and eager as he ever had. There were only the scratches now to show for his terrible experience aloft.

———

WHEN Charlie woke the next morning, he found Skrimville in a frenzy of excitement as it prepared to put into effect yet another plan. Mrs. Critch was all worked up and had already hauled the ladder out of the garage so Charlie could climb up on the roof. He could see ladders being hauled out all down the street.

"The hardware store has already sold out of black paint, Charlie. I got the last of it. Mr. Gross was mixing all the other colors together into five gallon buckets to make more black—or a kind of dirty gray. Eat your breakfast now so you can get up on the roof. Here—here is the picture you have to copy onto the shingles. Only you have to make it bigger, of course, so it looks like real bird shadows." The picture was a Xerox copy of a page from a bird guide, showing the silhouettes of eagles and hawks and other birds of prey. "The mayor made two hundred of these copies, to pass around. He says if we paint silhouettes on all the roofs to look like the shadows of those big birds flying over, it will scare the starlings away."

"It will?"

"Well—well, the mayor said it would. He said we should try it, Charlie."

"Nothing else has worked," Charlie said, buttering his toast. "Those birds aren't even afraid of cannon. What makes him think—"

"Well he *said*, the mayor *said*, that even if they're not afraid of cannon, every bird is afraid of a bigger bird that can grab him."

At Mrs. Critch's insistance, Charlie painted six eagle silhouettes across the roof. Then he took himself off to the dump as fast as he could before she decided she wanted more. All over Skrimville people were climbing around on their rooftops painting madly. Charlie had to grin. He wished Rory and Crispin could see the commotion. He bet those shadows painted on the roofs would look really impressive from the sky. Maybe, he thought, if the silhouettes really did frighten the starlings away, Rory and Crispin could fly the *Fox* right over Skrimville once to get the full effect of the rooftops—just before they took off on their trip.

But the thought of that trip made Charlie feel lonely suddenly. And he felt even worse when he arrived at the dump to find Rory and Crispin busily stowing supplies in the *Fox*. "But you can't go yet! You—you haven't practiced enough. You can't just go . . ."

"How can I practice," growled the kangaroo rat, "with starlings cluttering up the sky! I'll practice out there, away from Skrimville, sonny. We're going to take a cross-country flight. Every pilot has to do a hundred mile cross-country before he gets his license. I'll practice out there where the sky is free of all these flappin' nuisances."

"A cross-country?" Charlie knew very well that every pilot took a cross-country flight, a short first trip, before he was eligible for his license. A short trip from which he would return in a few hours. He hadn't thought about Rory doing that. "A cross-country?" he repeated stupidly.

"Well of course, sonny! Where've you been! I thought you knew all about flying!"

"Well I—well I—I think that's a great idea!"

"That's better, sonny. Now here's a grocery list, just a few things in case of emergency: raisins, some chocolate, a bit of jerky. I figured to start tomorrow, real early, before the starlings get out here. But now the flappin' radio says a rainstorm is headed this way, so we might have to wait. I found this map this morning," he said, indicating the map he had been standing on as he talked. "It looks to me like this little town here . . ." he pointed to Arden, which was just a hundred miles south, ". . . would be about right for our destination. Should take us about an hour to Jonesburg, another hour to Arden. Is this farm country in between, sonny?"

"That's all farm country."

"Good. We'll have to lay over a night for every gas stop. Can't very well siphon gas from a farmer's gas pump in the daytime. Should put us back in Skrimville four days after takeoff." The kangaroo

rat turned to checking his tools, laying aside those he would take, a couple of wrenches, a screwdriver. He looked up once, spied a starling flying in their direction, and whispered hastily to Charlie, "Don't say any more."

Charlie stared out at the starling. "But they can't understand us."

"What makes you think they can't?"

"But they—well my gosh, they don't ever talk!"

"They'd rather listen and *not* talk. It makes you more uncomfortable, don't it?"

Charlie guessed it did.

"I don't want them nosing around. It would be just like them to stay here all night, just to stop us from taking off," Rory whispered. "Wish we could lock every one of the flappin' critters in this hangar before we go!"

Charlie grinned. With that flock of starlings, it would take a bigger hangar than this one. It would take the big hangar at the airfield to hold all those birds.

"Maybe they won't be here," Charlie whispered. "Maybe the town's new plan will work after all."

"What plan, sonny? What are you talking about?"

"The silhouettes. The town is painting eagle and vulture shadows on the roofs like mad. If it works, Rory, those starlings will be a thousand miles from Skrimville by the time you take off in the morning." And then he paused and stared at Rory. "But if it doesn't work, and you have to take off before the starlings get to the dump then—well, you'll have to take off when it's still practically dark! You won't be able to see, you could run into a power line or . . ."

"It'll be all right, sonny. I'll go up real high and maybe circle a little until it gets light enough to see. It'll be all right, don't you worry about it."

18

W E L L before dusk, Skrimville's doorways and windows were lined with eager spectators, awaiting the arrival and then the frantic departure of the starlings as they swept over town, saw the threatening silhouettes, and rose in one last churning cloud. There was an air of surpressed eagerness among the crowd and whispers of a celebration.

Charlie and Mrs. Critch stood at the living room window, watching.

At dusk the birds came. They flew in from the dump in their usual manner, somewhat heavy and sluggish from stuffing themselves with garbage. They darkened the sky as if a giant hand had turned off the light. They hovered over the rooftops, ready to drop down and take over Skrimville.

And they rose at once, screaming hysterically at the sight of the painted shadows.

They hovered uncertainly in the sky, uttering questioning high whistles. They circled, looking down, heads cocked.

Then they looked up. They saw the empty sky

above them. They could see no eagles or vultures or hawks, nothing but clear sky turning slowly dark. They circled again, checked the sky again. Then they whistled bronx cheers and dropped down onto signboards and telephone wires screaming their defiance at Skrimville.

"Well, so much for that," Charlie said. Mrs. Critch shook her head with disappointment and went back to the kitchen.

The next morning Charlie got up well before dawn and went right on out to the dump. If the *Fox* was going to take off, he was going to be there to watch her. And to tell Rory the starlings hadn't left, so he could take off in plenty of time. But he found Rory and Crispin grunging around in the hangar, scowling and not at all ready to depart.

"The starlings didn't leave," he said. "What's the matter? Did you decide not to go? That it was too dangerous in the dark? But—"

"No, that ain't it, sonny. I'd have taken off all right. It's the weather. There are heavy winds over Arden heading this way and, the news said, bringing rain. I'd go if it were just me, sonny. But I don't like to endanger the *Fox*—and the lemming here."

"Is that the only reason?"

"Well, a good pilot isn't a foolish pilot," Rory added, making Charlie feel better.

Crispin was stretched out on his cot half-awake. He smiled as if he'd been dreaming something nice. "I made him some mint tea," Rory said. "The little fellow still seems kinda peaked."

"I'd be peaked too," Charlie said, "if some band of gangsters had tossed *me* around in the sky. Wish we could lock them up like gangsters."

Crispin woke and looked up at Charlie. "Why *don't* you lock them up, Charlie? We can't ever fly the *Fox* if they . . . I'm afraid to go up there in the sky with them there. Why *can't* you lock them up?"

"Sure, we'll just put them in the Skrimville jail," Charlie said. But something began to nag at him. Something Rory had said. He scowled at Rory, trying to remember. They had been talking about Rory's trip. Rory had said it would be just like the starlings to stop them from taking off. He had said—*that was it!* "*You* said it, Rory! *You* said what to do with them!"

"What, sonny? What did I say?"

"You said"—Charlie gulped with excitement—"you said, 'Wish we could lock every one in the hangar . . .'"

"Well I guess I did, sonny. But I don't—" Rory broke off and stared at Charlie. "The big hangar! Is that what you mean, sonny? The big hangar at the airfield?"

"That's exactly what I mean."

There was a long silence while everyone thought about that. At last Rory said, "It's crazy, sonny. It's too crazy to think about."

"Is it?" Charlie asked.

Rory began to pace, twirling the end of his tail. He began to get interested in the idea. He looked out into the dump and up onto the roof of the hangar. There were no starlings listening. Some minutes later they heard the flock flap noisily out from town. "If you could get those starlings to go into the big hangar, sonny," Rory said softly. "If you could get them to *want* to go in . . ."

"They came in here when it rained," Crispin said.

"The youngster's right," Rory said. "And a rainstorm's headed this way, a real doozy, the radio says. Would those birds go into the big hangar the same way they came in here? If they thought you didn't want them there . . ."

"They always crowd around the lights in town," Charlie said. "Maybe because it's warm there. We could turn the lights on in the hangar when it starts to rain . . ."

"And if you could make them think you didn't want them," Rory repeated, "if you could put up some kind of barricade that *looked* like you wanted to keep them out . . ."

"We could hang canvas drop cloths," Charlie said. "We could leave them loose, and not cover the whole door."

"And then, when they were all in, *slammo*, you shut the hangar door and you've got yourself a whole mess of starlings."

"And the drop clothes would keep them from getting out so fast while we were closing the doors."

"Oh my," Crispin said. "Then what will you do with them, Charlie? What will you do with them after you've trapped them all?"

119

Charlie and Rory looked at each other. What could you do with a hangar full of starlings?"

"Well at least they'd be out of the way," Charlie said. "They couldn't bother anyone. Except—except, my dad still couldn't open his repair shop."

"Yeah, sonny. It's your dad's hangar they'd be trapped in."

"I'll have to call him," Charlie said.

"What will he say, sonny?"

"I don't know. My gosh, Rory, I never thought of that."

CHAPTER
19

CHARLIE made the phone call from his dad's bedroom. Though he didn't think he had to worry about Mrs. Critch prying, she'd been so nice and thoughtful lately. As Rory said, "Don't worry about what's wrong with her, sonny. Just enjoy it while you can. You don't get a break like that every day."

His dad was staying in a boarding house and had to be called to the phone. "Is that you, Charlie?"

"Yeah, Dad, it's me."

"I was going to call you. You okay?"

"Sure. What were you going to call about?"

"You first."

"Well, okay. See, I had this idea about how to get rid of the starlings. But I need your permission. I found out they like to get in under shelter when it rains. And they like electric lights, because they're always snuggling up to them in town. Well, there's a rain storm due, and I thought—well, if we could move the planes out of the repair hangar and turn on the lights and open the hangar door, I think we could trap them in there."

"*What?* Trap that flock of dirty birds in my nice, clean hangar?"

"Well, Dad, I—"

"And shut the hangar door with them inside?"

"Well, I—"

"*Wow*, Charlie! I think you've hit on something!"

"You mean you like the idea?"

"Like it? It's crazy. It's wonderful. But Charlie?"

"Yes, Dad?"

"What're you going to do with them after you catch them?"

"Well see, Dad, that's the rub. I don't know. Only —well, they'd be *in* there. We're bound to think of something."

"Can you get anyone to help you get the planes out?"

"I think so."

"Put them around back as far from where those starlings will be flying as you can. And cover that little skyhawk, it has its cowling off."

"Yes, I will, Dad. *Wow! You like the idea!*"

"Sure I like it, what did you think? But you'd better be thinking hard about what to do afterward. You can't shoot them in there, Charlie. The hangar would be a sieve."

"I know."

"Besides, there's something sneaky and unfair about shooting anything in an enclosed place, even starlings. And you . . . well, I'll leave it to you,

Charlie. Sounds like you're onto something. Oh boy, my poor hangar. It'll look like a snowstorm hit it. Better get as much stuff into the office as you can, where it'll stay clean."

"Yes sir, I will. Engine parts and tools. We can hose the hangar down afterward. I'll go talk to the mayor. If you think of anything to do with the starlings when we've caught 'em, call me back, huh, Dad? And what were you going to call me about?"

"There's an air show up here in Allensville next weekend. They've asked me to serve as mechanic. I thought I'd run down and get you, if you'd like to go. Or you could take the train up."

"Well—well, yeah, Dad, I would like to," Charlie said hesitantly. Usually, there would be nothing he'd like better. But now . . . "If the starlings are all taken care of," Charlie said; and he thought, If Rory and Crispin get off on their cross-country all right. "Yeah, Dad, can I let you know later in the week, depending on the starlings?"

"Sure can. Let me know what happens."

20

―――――――

"B U T Charles, the town's last project to get rid of the starlings didn't work at all and I—"

"*Charlie*. I know, Mr. Leeper. It bombed out. But maybe this will be different. At least, it's worth a try. It won't be very much work, if we can get a couple of men to help me. And it isn't going to cost anything," Charlie added.

That part appealed to the mayor. A lot of expensive black paint had gone down the drain on the last project. Mayor Leeper considered, scowling down at Charlie. At last he scratched his ear. "All right, Chuck. I'll see what I can do. Maybe . . ."

"*Charlie*," Charlie corrected. "The pilots of the planes in the hangars would be the best ones to move them and get them tied down." Charlie didn't want a lot of bungling around and damage to the planes.

"You're right, Chet. Do you know any of those pilots?"

"*Charlie!* Sure, I know them all."

By one o'clock that afternoon every plane had been moved out of the repair hangar and tied down securely behind it. The skyhawk had been covered, and the tools and the engine parts had been moved into the little office, making it pretty crowded in there. According to the radio, the rainstorm was on its way. Already dark clouds were gathering over Skrimville as Charlie and the two pilots hung loose tarps over the hangar door. They left plenty of room between for the starlings to come in. Jerry wasn't much taller than Charlie, a slight, pale-haired man. He held Charlie's ladder while Charlie nailed up one end of a tarp and Joe, on the other ladder, nailed the other end. When they finished they settled down to wait for the rain. Joe and Jerry played poker with some cards from Charlie's dad's desk, and Charlie sat with his feet on the desk, thinking.

When he had gone home after seeing the mayor, he had discovered why Mrs. Critch had been so nice lately, and that needed thinking about.

He had heard the noise when he was still a block from home, a high-pitched wailing that made the hair on the back of his neck stand up. By the time he reached his house it was giving him a headache. It was coming from his house all right. He had pushed the door open and looked in.

There was no one in the living room. The noise was coming from the back of the house. Charlie went on back, and there in Mrs. Critch's little room stood her nephew Mush, his cheeks puffed out, blowing on a flute. Charlie stared. Mrs. Critch rushed in from the kitchen looking guilty. Mush smiled sheepishly, blew one last writhing note, and was still.

Mrs. Critch must have planned very carefully, to keep this secret hidden. Charlie could tell she was afraid he'd phone his dad. She almost cried as she tried to explain to Charlie. "You see, Charlie, they wouldn't—his mother wouldn't—let him practice at home. She says it gives her migraine. But the music teacher says Mush has a very unusual style and— well, there wasn't anywhere else for him to practice. He tried to practice at my house, but my other sister Maggie, she said she might be coming down with migraine too, if he didn't stop, and . . ." Mrs. Critch was really upset. "And so I let him practice here when you were gone. You've been gone so much I didn't think you'd find out." Mrs. Critch stopped talking and stared at him. "What are you going to do, Charlie? It's not Mush's fault, I told him he could . . ."

It gave Charlie a fine sense of power to have Mush and Mrs. Critch strung with apprehension over what he might do to them. He let them stew for a minute, and the minute stretched into a long, pregnant pause.

"You could . . ." Mrs. Critch said, "You could bring your—bring that animal back in the house, if you like, Charlie. I'm really sorry I made you . . ."

"It's too late for that," Charlie said sadly.

She looked pretty ashamed.

Finally he said, "It's okay, Mrs. Critch. Mush can practice here." He heard his own words and wondered if he'd lost his mind. He'd never heard of a boy his age having migraine, but he bet it was possible.

Now Charlie sat in his dad's office among the tools

and engine parts, watching the two pilots play poker and remembered that guilty look on Mush's face, and grinned. When he'd told Rory about it, Rory had said, "No wonder she didn't scold you for being gone so much. She was glad to have you out of there. Well, sonny, everyone has some talent. I guess old Mush found his."

"If that's a talent, I'll eat his flute. He sounds like a sick hyena." Charlie had stopped by the dump on his way to the airfield to move the planes and hang the canvas. There had been a half-dozen starlings pacing outside the hangar, obviously listening to Rory and Crispin and peering through the crack every few minutes. When Charlie removed the plywood, he found the two animals in a temper of impatience to be away from there and off on their cross-country flight—the *Fox's* maiden voyage. Of course they didn't say they were impatient, not wanting the starlings to hear. But they were so scowling and edgy, Charlie knew.

Held up by the coming rain, they had spread out some more maps across the hangar floor and, in faint whispers, were planning their long trip to see the world.

With the plywood removed, the starlings began to crowd right up to the edge of the map. So Charlie shoved the plywood back over most of the hangar, and blocked the rest with his back as he knelt to look in. Rory stared out past him muttering, "If it's going to rain I wish it'd get on with it!" Then, in a very faint whisper, "Now, sonny! Start talking!" And

Charlie winked at Rory and went into the whispering act they had planned, and his whispers were loud enough for the closest starlings to hear if they paid attention.

"We're going to try putting tarps over the hangar, I think that'll keep them out . . ."

"I don't know, sonny, they're pretty . . ."

"Oh, they won't fly in past those tarps," Charlie had whispered loudly.

"Well I wouldn't count on it, sonny, they . . ."

"My gosh, I hope they won't go in. Oh, they wouldn't, not a big hanger like that . . ."

Crispin had stared from one to the other in bewilderment. Then he had opened his mouth, and begun loudly, "But *you* said, Charlie . . ."

Rory had grabbed the lemming and slapped a paw over the little animal's mouth.

"I know what I said," Charlie ad-libbed quickly, "But we'll have to take a chance, that's all. Boy, if those starlings get in that hangar, they'll really ruin things."

The lemming had caught on at last, looked embarrassed, and was silent. Charlie had left soon afterward, mission accomplished. The starlings had overheard enough to make them hustle forward eagerly around the piano box, cocking their heads in puzzled interest, then flap away to tell their companions.

By one o'clock the big hangar was cleared and ready. By three o'clock the first few drops of rain had fallen, then stopped, and Jerry Wise had won three dollars and eighty-two cents from Joe Blake.

And by four thirty the first wave of birds was perched on top the hangar roof, to lean over the side and stare in with curious, beady eyes.

At last one scout entered the hangar. Immediately, Charlie ran out waving his arms and shouting as if he wanted to drive the bird away. The starling looked infuriated, swooped straight at Charlie's head, and landed on a rafter where he whistled derisively as he glared down at Charlie.

A few more birds came, eyeing Charlie insolently. Charlie made a big scene of running around waving the broom at them. The rain began again lightly.

Then suddenly, a whole platoon of birds scorched in, taking over the shelves and screaming harshly.

The rain began in earnest, and at that moment the entire flock of starlings suddenly wheeled off the roof, circled once, and stormed in through the canvas like an explosion to crowd around the hot lights and perch in droves on the rafters and shelves. The last birds to enter swept back and forth the length of the hangar fighting for perches. When they were all inside, bickering and hissing, Charlie and Jerry and Joe slipped out of the office and pulled the big hangar doors closed. The rain was really belting down.

They stood grinning at each other. They'd really done it, the birds were trapped in the hangar. They had lost maybe two dozen birds that had swept out at the last minute. But the rest of the starlings were in a passion of fury as they realized what had happened, and they began to dive and peck in an angry

attack; Charlie and the pilots nearly trampled each other getting through the office door and slamming it behind them.

"My gosh," Charlie said. "Are you guys okay?"

"We're fine," Joe Blake said. There was blood oozing from several peck marks near his scalp. His dark curly hair was streaked with blood.

Jerry Wise brushed some feathers from his pale hair. They stood looking at each other, and Charlie guessed they were all thinking the same thing because pretty soon Jerry said, "Now that we've got 'em, Charlie, what're we going to do with 'em?"

They discussed shooting the starlings and rejected that for the same reasons Charlie's dad had. They talked about pumping cyanide gas into the hangar, which would put the starlings to sleep quickly, and forever. But not one of them liked the idea.

"Besides," Joe Blake said, "this old building isn't that tight. The gas would leak out through the cracks around the doors and windows, and through that hole in the roof. It would take tons of gas."

"Seems to me," said Jerry Wise, pulling his tight tee-shirt tighter as he tucked it into his pants, "That that many starlings—that many of anything—ought to be worth something to someone. If you could just find a market for 'em."

"Who in the heck would want five thousand nasty-tempered starlings?" Joe Blake said laughing.

"They might make good dog food," Jerry said.

"Even if someone did want them, how would we get them to anybody?" Joe retorted. "A hangar full of starlings, and no way to crate them up and—"

"Crate them up!" they all said at once.

"Why not?" Charlie said. "Why not crate them?"

"Have to build the crates," Joe said. "Have to
. . ." He scratched his head, smearing blood. "And
how would we get them in there? With birdseed?"

"I don't know," Charlie said. "I guess they're too
smart to fall for birdseed all right. We'd have to make
them want to go in, just like with the hangar . . ."

"Why wouldn't birdseed work?" Jerry asked. "If
we started feeding 'em every day in a certain place
and got them used to that, *then* brought a couple of
empty crates in, put the crates in the feeding place,
and put the seed inside."

"It might work," Charlie said. "It just might . . ."

They left the hangar through the side door in the
little office, drove into town in Joe's jeep, and
rounded up all the birdseed there was to be had in
Skrimville, putting it on the city's charge accounts,
with Mayor Leeper's reluctant permission. They
cleaned out the grocery, the hardware, and the pet
store. The store owners were delighted because wild
bird feed hadn't been selling very well lately. Charlie
drove back with Joe, and they dropped some seed in
the hangar, receiving a dozen more pecks for their
trouble, then stored the rest in the office. Mean-
while, in town, Jerry Wise organized a building
crew, and by the time Charlie got back, he could
hear the whine of skill saws and the ring of hammers,
as Skrimville began to turn out crates for the starlings.

The mayor said, "Well Chester, I see you have

those starlings locked up. Once you get them into the crates, where do you think we should send them?"

"Charlie! My name's Charlie! I don't know where we should send them, Mr. Leeper. But it had better be a long way away."

21

───────────

"SEND 'em to China," Rory said. Charlie was sitting on his bike outside the piano box. He had pulled the plywood to one side so the sun could shine in— it was sunny for the first time in two days, though water still dripped from everything, for the rain had ceased only late in the afternoon. The two animals had the *Fox* packed and were all prepared for their cross-country. "Send 'em to China," Rory repeated. "I heard once that people in China eat fried larks, so maybe they'd like fried starlings."

The starling crates had all been built, forty-two big wooden crates. Five of them stood right now inside the mechanic's hangar, open and liberally scattered with seed. It had taken some doing to get the crates in through a crack in the big doors, and they had lost maybe another dozen starlings. But when Charlie had left the hangar, the first birds were already beginning to eat, flying in one at a time to snatch up a beakful of seed.

The dozen birds that had escaped, plus those that had escaped the first time, made an angry little band that sat now along the top of a pile of twisted bed springs, watching the piano box.

"I don't think you should take off with *them* out there," Charlie whispered softly.

"We can't stay here forever, sonny. The *Fox* needs to be flying. And I'm getting itchy feet."

"I still think you should practice more."

"I'll practice on the flight," Rory growled. "I plan to take off first thing in the morning, before it's light, be out of here before those starlings come. Will you nail the hangar up good when we're gone?"

"Maybe I'll put hinges on the plywood, and a latch."

"That'd be great, sonny. Except when we come back it'll only be for a day or so, to tune up the engine if she needs it, get ready for the long flight. Don't seem worthwhile to go to all that trouble just for that short time."

"I'll come out in the morning and take the plywood off anyway," Charlie said rather sadly. "And put it back afterward."

When Charlie got home, dinner wasn't quite ready and Mush was still practicing, so he shut himself in his room and lay on the bed trying to think of someone who might want a hangar full of starlings. Finally, he stuffed some cotton in his ears to block out Mush's playing, though it didn't help much. As he stared idly out the window, the three dozen starlings circled the house next door and landed on its roof.

"If we don't get rid of those three dozen, too,"

the mayor had said, "they'll breed and multiply into a thousand more before you can blink, Charles." Charlie wished they *could* send the whole stupid flock to China. The starlings on the roof next door seemed unusually quiet, were not quarreling, weren't even paying attention to the street lights that had just come on. They were crowded on the roof as close to Charlie's house as they could get, peering over at it. A few flew over to his roof, where he could not see them. Then suddenly the rest swooped down close to Charlie's window, wheeled, and landed on the sill fluttering against the glass.

What were they doing? They fluttered and wriggled as if they wanted to get in. Were they after him, for Pete's sake? Did they realize he was the one who had trapped the others in the hangar? Then suddenly, the birds lifted like ashes in an updraft and disappeared around the corner of the house. Charlie rose and went down the hall, trying to see them through other windows.

When he got to Mrs. Critch's room where Mush was playing, the starlings had crowded onto the windowsill and were pushing and flapping against the glass. Did Mush's playing madden them so their only thought was to get at Mush himself?

When Mush went home, the starlings left. Had the birds really wanted to attack him? Charlie watched him go quietly down the street, his flute hidden in its case, and there wasn't a starling near.

Mrs. Critch called Charlie to dinner, and she had the TV on. They watched the news idly as they ate.

Halfway through dinner the announcer gave the details of a disaster to the farming country west of Allensville.

". . . in the state capital, ladies and gentlemen. A disaster that will cripple the economy of the state for some time to come, and create hardship . . ." The camera panned in on a wheatfield; but a sick-looking wheatfield that seemed to be writhing in some kind of death throes as if the stalks were alive, crawling— crawling with grasshoppers. "Yes, ladies and gentlemen, this ravaging army of insects moved into Allensville last night and is playing havoc with the state's finest economic resource. The wheat stalks are literally alive with grasshoppers, stripping the stalks with their sharp teeth as they climb and swarm— chomping and digesting thousands of dollars worth of wheat in just the time we have been viewing them. There is no end in sight. The governor . . ."

Charlie forgot to eat, he was so interested. When the announcer said, "This part of the country does not have nearly enough robins and blackbirds to eradicate this menace. Why, it would take a veritable *army* of big, hungry birds to . . ." Charlie nearly jumped out of his chair.

As soon as the announcement was over, the phone began to ring.

Jerry Wise called first. "Why, we can ship those starlings up to Allensville, Charlie! They ought to pay plenty to save their crops."

Joe Blake called a few minutes later to say the same thing.

138

The mayor called. "Chadwick, this is wonderful news! We'll get a band of trucks together and haul those starlings up to Allensville in the morning!"

"But they . . ." But the mayor had hung up.

The next time the phone rang, it was Dad. "Think you can get those starlings crated by morning, Charlie? I drove out a few minutes ago to look at the grasshoppers, and they're the biggest, juiciest grasshoppers you ever saw! Those starlings would have a picnic; they'd never go back to Skrimville— if you can just get them here. Those farmers are frantic—do you think you could go down tonight, get the starlings in the crates, and have them ready for the trucks to start out early in the morning?"

"I don't know, Dad. Well, there's one thing we haven't tried. See, I *think* I've discovered a way to attract them. Only I'm not sure; it might just drive them into a temper. But—but I can't think of anything else, so I'll try it. But what trucks, Dad?"

"The trucks that are on their way down to Skrimville. They're just leaving. Every farm truck in the area is headed your way, to haul starlings."

"Oh my gosh," Charlie said, and hung up. When he had collected himself, he called the mayor. Then he called Jerry Wise and Joe Blake. And then he took off for Mush's house, hoping that flute would do what he thought it could do.

By nine o'clock they were all crowded into the little office among the motor parts and tools: Joe Blake, Jerry Wise, the mayor, Charlie, and Mush and his flute.

And by midnight Charlie's great plan had failed. Failed dismally. By midnight every hissing, evil starling was perched for the night on Skrimville's rooftops once again, and they looked as if they planned to stay forever.

Charlie sat alone in his dad's dark office, feeling miserable.

It had started out so well. They had pulled one of the crates up so its back was against the closed office door, and its opening facing the hangar. Charlie and Joe Blake had crouched in the hangar beside it, while inside the office Mush began to play. They all held their breaths—except Mush of course—not knowing whether the starlings would be lured into the box or would explode in a passion of fury.

At first the birds had stopped quarreling, grown quiet, and sat staring toward the office and the crate from which Mush's playing seemed to issue. Slowly their expressions had changed from evil to a mindless pleasure, as if they had been drugged. Then one bird swooped down and circled the crate. Then another. The flute bleated. Then a mass of starlings dropped suddenly, to crowd right into the crate, scrabbling and pushing as though they wanted to get through the back to Mush. Charlie and Joe grabbed the lid, pushed it over the crate, and nailed it down. Then they moved the crate as fast as they could and shoved another in its place.

Mush played on, and the starlings kept coming.

They had nailed up the third crate when Jerry Wise and the mayor slipped out of the office to help.

The nailing and the moving of crates upset the birds, but they would come right back as soon as things calmed down—as long as Mush played. But now with two more men there, the birds hesitated. These men were standing, not crouching out of the way. And the mayor was pretty big. As they moved the fourth crate into place, the birds gave them wide clearance; and then suddenly, inside the office, Mush stopped playing.

"Keep it up!" Charlie hissed through the wall. "Keep playing!"

"I'm tired, Charlie. I just need to rest my lips a minute. And I'm thirsty."

"I said, keep playing!" Charlie growled frantically. Mush started again, halfheartedly. But something had happened to the starlings. They were not mesmerized any more. They perched on the rafters, leering down in their normal, nasty way. They heard their companions flapping and hissing inside the closed crates. They whistled, and their crated companions whistled back. And the starlings on the rafters straightened their ranks, and suddenly a mass of starlings swept right at Charlie and the men, beating wings into faces, pecking. Charlie couldn't see, could hardly breathe. He tried to get the office door clear of the crate. The mayor was cornered between crates. "Get them off me, Chester! They'll kill me! Get your dratted birds off!" Charlie beat at the birds, but it was like trying to bail the ocean. "Open the door, Chuck! Open that hangar door and get them out of here! And stop that infernal flute!"

Charlie could hardly move for starlings. He felt Joe's hand on his arm and followed Joe blindly as the pilot tried to get the mayor into the office and as starlings beat and swept against them—then suddenly the mayor broke free, was swerving toward the big hangar door, swinging wildly back on the handle, pulling it . . .

"Oh no!" Charlie cried. "Oh, don't!"

But it was too late. The starlings saw a crack in the door and they swept out like a tide, into the moonlit sky.

The hangar was empty.

Charlie stared at Joe and Jerry. They all stared at the Mayor. Charlie began to feel really bad. Mush looked bewildered and opened a warm Coke.

In the morning, Allensville's trucks would be there, and Skrimville had only three crates of starlings to offer them at the end of their long drive. Charlie's plan had failed. The starlings were loose again in Skrimville. Charlie and Jerry and Joe were scratched and bleeding and full of feathers and bird droppings. So was the mayor, and mad as hops besides. When Mush started to play a tune to cheer them, the mayor nearly broke the flute over his head.

Everyone left but Charlie. The hangar was a terrible mess. Charlie stood staring at it for a few minutes feeling hopeless, then he turned out the lights and sat in the dark thinking grim thoughts.

142

CHAPTER
22

CHARLIE didn't go home, he was too depressed. He curled up under an old pair of coveralls in his dad's office, slept fitfully, and about four A.M. got up and made his way down the moonlit airstrip to the dump. The breeze was chilly. The tall grass at the edge of the airstrip caught the moonlight. The world seemed very deserted at four in the morning. Charlie's head ached.

There was a light in the piano box, and Rory and Crispin were up and eager to be off, now the rain had passed. They were waiting for him to remove the plywood. "If I hadn't come, what would you have done?" he asked grumpily.

"Wrenched it off ourselves, sonny! What else?"

Charlie told them about the starlings' escape. The animals listened silently. Rory turned away to make a few last adjustments to the *Fox*, then looked up at Charlie. "Listen, sonny, don't you worry about them starlings. At least you have those three crates to send up to Allensville. But I have a hunch, sonny—just a hunch, that them starlings'll all be gone from here soon."

Charlie tried to look hopeful, even though he knew the kangaroo rat was just trying to cheer him. "Well," he said with as much life as he could manage, "well maybe you're right, Rory." He forced himself to smile. "You'll be in Jonesburg tonight. That'll be great!"

"No, sonny. We'll be in Charmin tonight. And in Allensville tomorrow night."

"Allensville? But I thought you were going south."

"Well, there's the air show in Allensville, sonny. We thought we'd just take a look at it," the kangaroo rat said hastily, and turned away again to adjust the rudder trim tab of the *Fox*, which he had already done twice.

Charlie carried the *Fox* out to the airstrip just as the first faint hint of dawn touched the night sky. The moon had set. He put the plane down on the wide, empty asphalt and Rory climbed into the front cockpit.

"Listen, be careful up there until it gets light," Charlie said. "Just circle the field until you can see something, for gosh sakes!"

"I'll be careful, sonny. Come on, Crispin, give that prop a spin!"

Charlie stepped back. Crispin spun the prop and ducked away. The *Fox* roared, then purred as Rory retarded the spark. Crispin climbed into the back cockpit and strapped himself down.

Rory let the engine warm up, then taxied out to

the center of the big strip. Charlie could hardly see the *Fox* in the dark. Rory revved the engine awhile, then suddenly Charlie heard him let the *Fox* go, saw her dark shape speed down the runway, saw her lift into the dark sky and disappear almost at once.

And then he heard the hissing, quarreling approach of the starlings coming from town. He held his breath. Would they see the *Fox* and go after her?

But he guessed they didn't see her, because they settled noisily onto the garbage dump. Charlie breathed a sigh of relief. He stood there for quite a while as the sky lightened, gazing off in the direction the *Fox* had taken. The sky was completely empty.

It was going to be a dreary four days until Rory and Crispin returned.

Born aloft on the dawn wind, the *Fox* purred sweetly as she sped away from Skrimville. Pilot and passenger gazed around them at the slowly lightening sky and looked down at the brightening land below them. The stars began to fade. A wash of red reached up from the horizon to push back the darkness. Below them, the hills and meadows emerged, then gave way to plowed fields and winding roads. Each detail of the land fitted perfectly to the next, stream to hill, road to field or wood. A few tiny cars crawled along. Crispin forgot the fear of his first look downward and leaned over the side to stare in fascination as the mounting light picked out more and more of the countryside. And as the *Fox* winged on, the sky turned golden, then a deep blue. The clouds were like

snow mountains, like icebergs. And there were caverns among the clouds; Rory rolled the *Fox* and played among the clouds, getting a finer feel of the controls, of what the *Fox* could do. And grinning from ear to ear as she responded to him. He learned what her stall speed felt like. He learned to recover from an accelerated stall, the words from the flight manual flashing jumbled through his mind as he thought he had lost control, then felt her respond and straighten out. He knew quite well he was doing more than he should. But he was up there in the *Fox*, and he had no one to help him learn but his own common sense and memory. He wished several times that he did have a flight instructor aboard, though he would never have admitted it to Charlie. And the feel of flying, of the plane under him, was like nothing in the world he had known. He was nearly drunk with the pleasure of it.

Crispin forgot his giddiness at the steep banks. Or perhaps he grew to like it. He laughed with pleasure as the *Fox* rolled.

And too soon their hour was all but gone, their fuel running low, and Rory was circling a lone farm south of Charmin, looking for a flat place to land.

Charlie mooched around his room feeling unsettled. He threw away some ancient Hershey wrappers and some bent nails. Where were Rory and Crispin now? They had to have landed by this time. They would be out of gas.

Well, they were all right. Charlie fished half a

dozen chewed socks out of the bottom of his bed and sat looking at them. Then he spread up the covers and finally went down the hall to phone his dad and say he didn't feel like going up to the air show. He said he guessed he'd just grunge around his room and maybe give it a good cleaning. He had thought about trying to find Rory and Crispin at the air show, but the *Fox* would be landing at Skrimville Sunday morning. If he went to the air show, he wouldn't be back until late Sunday night. He wished he were with them. He wished . . .

"Charlie, are you still on the phone?"

"Sure, Dad. I'm here."

"Listen, Charlie, it isn't going to do you any good to lounge around there feeling wiped out. I know how you feel about the starlings, but it couldn't be helped, that's all. You did the best you could. Charlie, this is Thursday, and if you hop on that late train tomorrow night, you can be up here by ten o'clock. We can catch what there is of the air show. Though some of it has been canceled because of the grasshopper plague. No one up here is much in the mood for entertainment. But what do you say? Feel like coming? I could use the company. It gets pretty lonely up here."

Charlie swallowed. "I—I'll see you tomorrow night at ten."

He threw a pair of socks and a sweater in his flight bag and tossed it on the bed. Then he went out across the uncut lawn, got his bike, and headed for the dump. There was no place else he really wanted to be.

When he got there he collected junk for a while, then, at last, he took the plywood off the hangar, found some hinges for it, and rehung it. He fiddled around for a long time, installing a latch and getting it to work so the animals could open it. Both hinges and latch were plenty rusty. He had forgotten to bring anything to eat, and in midafternoon, when his stomach was starting to growl, he closed up the hangar, picked up his bike, and was about to throw a leg over when a tiny noise stopped him cold.

He looked up at the sky. He strained to see. There was a humming somewhere out there in the vast sky, a tiny purr like a bee. And it was getting louder. And it was not a bee. It was an engine, it had to be an engine. But it was too high-pitched for a big plane.

Charlie could see a speck now. It was—it *had* to be. He started running toward the airstrip.

Why were they coming back? What was wrong?

When he reached the strip, the speck was bigger. He could see color now. It *was* the *Fox!* He could almost see her markings. Yes! Soon he could see pilot and passenger waving.

He stood on the asphalt gawking as Rory circled in pattern—and as the starlings rose in a black angry mass from the garbage dump and sped up toward the little plane, whistling a challenge. Charlie screamed and waved and ran, trying to frighten them away. The *Fox* turned and flew right at them. *"Oh don't Rory! Get away from them!"* Charlie yelled.

The starlings were almost at the plane, some beginning to circle her—she would be surrounded in another second. And the lemming—the lemming was standing up in the cockpit! He had removed his seat harness and was standing almost on top of the plane holding onto the upper wing. What was the fool animal doing? He'd fall; starlings were diving at him viciously. What was he holding up above his head? Something half as big as he was. The starlings had paused in flight when, with one tremendous throw, Crispin pitched the object up and away from the plane. Two starlings swooped, snatched at it, and were tearing it apart between them as the others crowded around them. With the birds fighting among themselves above her, the *Fox* came in to land.

She had almost landed when some starlings broke away from the squabbling crowd and dove at her. Again Crispin stood up and threw something high in the air—and again the starlings ignored the plane in their eagerness to snatch it out of the air.

The *Fox* was on the ground at last. She taxied up to Charlie. He stood over her, trying to protect her as the starlings began again to dive.

_____

"W H A T were you *doing* up there?" Charlie yelled. "What were you throwing out of the plane? How come you're home so soon? What . . ." The *Fox* sat safely on the runway. The starlings whistled and hovered close above, watching her intently. "What were you throwing out of the plane?" Charlie repeated. What . . ."

"Shh, sonny," Rory said in a fake whisper, "Shhh. Let's get these things out of here and into a safe place. We've already tossed away two, just to get down safe. I don't want to lose any more."

Now Charlie could see that Crispin had been sitting jammed into a small corner of the rear cockpit, and a bulging cloth bag took up most of the space. It towered high above the seat, and it almost looked alive the way it wiggled and writhed.

"But . . ."

"Shh, sonny," Rory whispered loudly as starlings dropped down to listen. "Shoo those birds out of here. Listen, sonny, these are the biggest, juiciest grasshoppers you ever tasted. And we've found an unlimited supply! Unlimited, sonny. Grasshoppers as far as the eye can see." His whisper was hoarse and carrying. The starlings cocked their heads and their eyes sparkled. Rory, his back to them, winked broadly at Charlie. "We had some fried this noon, sonny, and I tell you—"

"*Grasshoppers?*"

"Shhhh, sonny! My gosh, use your head. They'll have every one if we don't get out of here fast. Come on, sonny, see if you can get this bag of grass-hoppers to the hangar before we lose any more."

Charlie grinned, picked up the *Fox*, grasshoppers, pilots and all, and made a dash for the piano crate with starlings swooping around him.

When the plane was safe inside, he crawled inside himself and pulled the plywood door closed. They could hear the starlings outside crowding and hissing as they pushed up to the crate to listen and peer in.

"Now tell me," Charlie whispered just loud enough for them to hear. "How the heck did you find such terrific grasshoppers?"

"Have a look, sonny. They really are sensational." Rory pushed the bag toward Charlie. Beady eyes watched. Charlie opened the bag and lifted out a fat, wriggling grasshopper. The starlings sighed. Charlie opened the bag again, and a second grasshop-per leaped past his fingers and was free.

"Catch him!" Rory cried, and dove after the grass-hopper, chasing it skillfully toward the crack in the door where it slipped through quick as lightning— and was snatched up and fought over noisily. The three friends grinned at each other.

When the birds had ceased quarreling and were pressing once more against the door, Rory whispered, "I'm going to bag these critters up and sell 'em, sonny. Why there's all we can eat and a million times more than that. I could fill a whole fleet of planes with grasshoppers. The most succulent things fried you ever tasted." And then, in a much lower whisper that the starlings couldn't possibly hear, "Ask me *where*, sonny! For gosh sakes, ask me *where!*"

"Where in heck did you find them?" Charlie whispered loudly. "My gosh, Rory, it's as good as discovering gold. Where did you find so many?"

"Up to Allensville, sonny. Why, they're as thick as a carpet up there. We were flying along nice as you please, when we looked down and saw the ground was *covered* with grasshoppers, a whole army of them chomping on the wheat, hopping around . . ." The starlings sighed again. "Well sonny, we flew right down and landed, and we began snatching grasshoppers off the wheat stalks right and left. They were so thick you couldn't even walk between them. Oh, we had us a feast—what a feast . . ." Rory reached into the bag and pulled out another grasshopper. It did look juicy, all right. "Right up in Allensville, sonny, not two hours flight from here as straight north as a fellow can go. Lies just west of a long line of hills," he whispered loudly, shoving the grasshopper safely back into the bag.

"But how did you make it clear to Allensville and

back in one day?" Charlie asked finally. "I thought . . ."

"Luck, sonny," the kangaroo rat said lightly. There was no need to whisper now, though the starlings still pressed close around the edges of the plywood. "Just pure luck. Our first refueling was at a farm outside Charmin the way we planned. We landed, located the gas pump, and hid the plane to wait 'til dark. We could smell breakfast cooking and could see the family inside the farmhouse. Well sonny, when they'd finished up their breakfast, the farmer and his wife and three kids locked the house, locked up the chickens, chained up the dog, got in their truck and drove away. Pretty soon the smoke from the chimney died, so we guessed there wasn't anyone else at home. The gas pump was just beside the barn. There were even a couple of oil cans near it. We thought about cats but decided to take a chance.

"Well I'll tell you, sonny, that old German shepherd just about tore that chain out by the roots when we took off at the edge of the woods, circled the *Fox* real low, and came in just beside the gas pump. He couldn't figure out what we were, or what we were doing, but he darn sure knew we shouldn't be there. We tipped some oil into that measuring cup we carried along, and when we'd got enough oil into the tank, Crispin climbed the gas pump and flipped the switch. It took just a second to fill up the *Fox*'s tank. But that hose adapter we made didn't work so well, we spilled a lot of gas. The next time we did it all different. Anyway, spilled a lot of gas, had to wipe the *Fox* off from prop to tail, with that dog having apoplexy not six yards from us. When we took off again, he was still lunging at the end of his chain, and he'd woke up the cats, but they were a stupid lot. They didn't like the smell of gas and were all pacing around lashing their tails, but they wouldn't come near the plane. Well we just revved up the *Fox* and took off, and that put us clear up to Allensville in just under three hours, and there were those flappin' grasshoppers just writhing and wriggling and waiting for someone to come along and sample them . . ."

There was a big rasping sigh from the starlings.

"You had it all planned!" Charlie whispered very faintly. "You went up to Allensville on purpose!"

Rory grinned.

"And in Allensville, sonny, everything was in such an uproar that it wasn't hard at all to locate a tractor left standing alone in a field and siphon out some gas. That farmer's going to be pretty surprised when he finds a dollar bill and a note under a rock on his tractor seat. We had to take oil from a can in his utility box behind the seat, so we left him a note telling him to check it—so he wouldn't run out, sonny, and get caught oilless. At the farm back in Charmin we'd just tossed the money up on top the gas pump. That farmer'll probably think he put it there himself."

"And coming back, Charlie," Crispin said, "we stopped at the very same farm! I was scared to, but Rory said . . . well, the truck wasn't back yet, and the cats had gone to sleep. That old dog sure barked, though. If that chain had ever broken . . ."

It was about that time that they heard a different kind of stirring outside the hangar. The birds had stopped crowding around the plywood, and when Charlie looked out, they had begun to leave. First in threes and fours, then by the dozens, and at last in black knots of birds. And they were not returning to the garbage dump. Nor were they heading for town, or for the pine grove. They were rising straight up into the sky as if bent on some serious mission. They rose very swiftly for starlings, and silently; and, high over the dump, they gave a great whistle of mocking derision, hissed rudely, and set off on a northerly course as fast as starlings could go.

Charlie stared at Rory. Rory stared at Charlie. They both looked at the lemming, whose whiskers had begun to twitch. And they all began to grin.

By four o'clock that afternoon there was not a starling left in Skrimville or anywhere near it. Not at the garbage dump, not in the pine woods, not in town. And at seven o'clock, when Charlie got home for dinner, the word was on TV.

". . . like a miracle, ladies and gentlemen. Here in Allensville people are crowding the roads that lead out to the wheatfields, trying to catch a glimpse of the spectacle. The farmers are jubilant. All the churches are open for special thanksgiving. The black cloud of starlings swept in here late this afternoon and began gobbling grasshoppers by the bushelful. At this rate, ladies and gentlemen, it is estimated that nearly half the state's wheat crop may be saved. Now here, live from the scene, is our camera crew and John Mooney . . ." The shot panned to John Mooney, then narrowed in on a wheatfield black with starlings diving and screaming as they gorged themselves on giant grasshoppers. The camera zoomed in for some closeups, and the birds could be seen gulping down wriggling grasshoppers as fast as they could swallow. "I've never seen anything like it, ladies and gentlemen . . ." John Mooney was saying.

Mrs. Critch got so interested in the television, she burned the spaghetti sauce. She and Charlie and Mush were crowded around the TV. During dinner the phone rang twelve times.

Joe Blake shouted, "Turn on your TV, Charlie. My gosh, the starlings have really left Skrimville!"

Jerry Wise said, "I knew it! Could have made us a nice pile, selling those starlings to the farmers up in Allensville! Drat the luck!"

The mayor screamed, "It's a miracle, Chauncy! A true miracle!"

When Dad called, he said, "Hey Charlie, did you have something to do with putting the starlings onto those grasshoppers?"

"Me, Dad? How could I do such a thing?"

"I don't know, but I had a funny feeling you might. Isn't it great!"

"It's terrific, Dad."

"Are you coming up tomorrow night?"

"I sure am!"

"Good. See you then. And I have a surprise for you."

"What is it?"

"I said a *surprise*, Charlie Gribble! See you at ten."

24

O N Friday morning the *Fox* took off on her long journey. Rory had stocked her with raisins and jerky, though they meant to live mostly off the land. Charlie had noticed a pilot doll in the dime store and had bought two of the flight helmets for it, to wrap up as going-away presents. The kangaroo rat and the lemming looked rakish in the helmets. "Like barnstormers, sonny! Like a couple of real old barnstormers!"

"Have a good time," Charlie shouted as the *Fox* revved her motor.

"We'll write to you, sonny."

"*Write* to me?"

"Sure, sonny," the kangaroo rat shouted. "There're post offices, aren't there? You've heard of mailboxes, haven't you?

"But how . . ." Charlie shouted, running alongside the taxiing *Fox*, "How can I write you back?"

"General delivery, sonny! I can slip under the door of any post office in the country!"

The *Fox* roared, lifted, was skyborne while Char-

lie was still running; she purred above him, circling, as the two animals waved. She tilted her wings once, then headed south straight as an arrow.

Charlie stood staring after her until she was out of sight. And just before she disappeared, he saw another flying shape join her, and another—five big birds, wing for wing, in an undulating flight that followed for some seconds, as if in farewell, then veered off to the right.

The flicker had found his family. And the *Fox* was off on the most wonderful adventure any animal had ever imagined. Charlie stood there in the middle of the deserted runway and stared at the empty sky for a long time.

The air show was a big success. The people of Allensville were in such a good mood after the arrival of the starlings that they turned out in droves, crowding the grandstand and setting up batteries of folding chairs. The press and television reporters who had come to cover the arrival of the starlings stayed to cover the air show, and the publicity the air show got made everyone even happier.

But Charlie's dad's surprise was, to Charlie, the best part of all. And it was such a crazy, impossible surprise, that Charlie couldn't wait to write to Rory about it.

It was a week before Charlie received a letter from Rory so that he knew where to write.

Dear Sonny,
Here we are in Smithson, only a hundred miles

away, and it's taken us three days to get here! First thing, some fool eagle took us for a flappin' bird and almost tore our wing off before he realized his mistake. And then, on our second gas stop, we had to haul the gas in a bucket clear across a pasture in the middle of the night, and the farm cat nearly got Crispin.

"Well, anyway, here we are at last in Smithson. Not much of a town, but the flying has been great. The Fox flies like a dream, if I do say so myself. And yesterday I let the youngster sit up in the front cockpit with me. There's just room if you don't mind crowding. I let him work the controls a little bit.

We plan to be in Falter at the end of next week, so you could write to us there % General Delivery, if you have time.

Your friend,
Rory

And Crispin added at the bottom;

Dear Charlie,

It's wonderful! Everything is so little down there. And the clouds are real, Charlie. They're like towers in the sky! We fly around them, and sometimes even on top of them! It's like sailing on the wind, Charlie. And one time a big airplane flew by above us and turned around and came right down and looked at us. That scared me. But it's wonderful all the same, and I wish you could be here with us.

Love,
Crispin

163

Charlie wrote back, % General Delivery, Falter:

Dear Rory and Crispin and the Fox,
You'll never guess what happened. Never! *Do you remember Mary Starr Colver, and that she is a famous pilot? Well, she was at the air show. That was my dad's surprise. She got to talking to him, and when she found out his name was Gribble, she said she knew another Gribble, from Skrimville, and she told him about the parts I'd written for, and he said that had to be Charlie Gribble, and she said yes it was. She had taken her models to Allenville to fly as a benefit for an air school she wants to open for homeless kids. And do you know why she collects models? You'd think someone who can fly wouldn't bother about models. But Mary Starr Colver can't fly any more. She crashed her Mooney 201 three years ago in the Reno Air Races, and she has to be in a wheelchair now. She crashed it because of something faulty in the engine. She can still get into a plane, though, and a friend of hers flew her up to Allensville. And —well, you won't believe this part! Do you remember the plane that passed you close by after you left Skrimville? The one that came back to have another look? Well I told you you wouldn't believe it, but that was Mary Starr Colver, flying with her friend. They saw you. They saw the* Fox, *and Miss Colver said, "That can't be a radio control, look, there's no antennae!" So they banked around, and she told me she thought she was cracking up because she could have sworn she saw two (please pardon the expres-*

sion) mice flying that plane, and she said she even thought they were wearing flight helmets.

Her friend accused her of drinking, and then he laughed. But Mary Starr Colver saw you! And she said that the funniest thing about it was, the plane was a Fairey Fox. That was one reason she told me about it. She said there weren't all that many models of the Fairey Fox. She looked at me real funny when she said it, but I didn't say anything. I just grinned kind of stupidly and asked her if she had been drinking.

Write soon and let me know where you are. Mrs. Critch saw the envelope of your letter in the mail, and she said she guessed I had a girl friend at last, and didn't she have small handwriting!

Your friend and love,
Charlie Gribble